CHRISTMAS LIGHTS AND SNOWBALL FIGHTS

LITTLE BAMTON BOOK 1

BETH RAIN

Copyright © 2020 by Beth Rain

Christmas Lights and Snowball Fights (Little Bamton Book 1)

First Publication: 9th November, 2020

All rights reserved.

No part of this book may be reproduced in any form or by any electronic or mechanical means, including information storage and retrieval systems. Except for use in any review, the reproduction or utilization of this work, in whole or in part, in any form by any electronic, mechanical or other means now known or hereafter invented, is forbidden without the written permission of the publisher.

Published by Beth Rain. The author may be contacted by email on
bethrainauthor@gmail.com

CHAPTER 1

*S*tupid sucky work. Stupid sucky Christmas.

Caro Jenkins leant back in the cramped seat of her little red Nissan Micra and attempted to stretch her back.

Okay, okay - she'd take that last bit back. She didn't *hate* Christmas but working in retail had a habit of beating the festive joy out of you, and this year was always going to be a difficult one considering what happened last Boxing Day. But she wasn't going to think about that right now. No way. She had her Christmas Spotify playlist blaring out her favourites - none of which featured on the CD that had been on auto-repeat in the shop since October. It might be a high-end boutique where women of a certain age came to buy their over-priced clothes, but the owner was far too stingy to spring for a new CD. So, she'd had to put up with the same sixteen songs on a loop for the past five Christmases.

Caro sighed. Five years. She should have been out of there by now. Her dream had always been to own her own business - a little cave of vintage gorgeousness that she could fill with whatever she fell in love with as well as her own up-cycled creations. But she'd never quite had the money to make her dream come true. Well, apart from last year when she'd been so close she could almost smell it. Of course, that's when her life imploded and screwed everything up.

'CARO!' she huffed at herself in the chilly confines of the car, trying to stop her brain from circling that particular thought-drain again. She hastily reached out, cranked up the heating and sang a couple of lines along with Sia to cheer herself up.

'Stay on the A38 for ... 15 miles.'

'Rude!' Caro snapped at the Google Maps automated voice for interrupting her impromptu festive karaoke.

She hated that she had to rely on a Satnav to get her safely to her parents' house less than thirty miles away, but she'd resigned herself to the fact that she had zero sense of direction a long time ago. Even with the annoyingly smug voice of the Google lady in her ear, she'd taken a gazillion trips around the large roundabout on the way out of Plymouth.

Her non-existent sense of direction had always been a source of tension between her and Gareth, her ex. He'd been such a stickler for getting everything right and being everywhere on time. He'd completely freaked out every time she got lost - which was basically every time they got in the car together. There was something about his huffy, sanctimonious expectation that she was going to take a wrong turning eventually that always made sure that it became a self-fulfilling prophesy.

By the time the Google lady had told her to take a u-turn back to the roundabout for the fifth time, Caro told her in no uncertain terms to fuck the fuck off. Gareth had always loved the Google lady. Maybe that's why Caro hated her quite so much.

It was a question she'd asked herself over and over again in the year since their relationship had blown up quite so spectacularly - had Gareth *become* a twat while they were together? Or had he always been like that, and she'd just failed to notice because of her stupid, rose-tinted love-specs? She wasn't sure which answer she preferred, if she was honest. Either way, she was glad she was shot of him, and if she repeated it to herself often enough, maybe - one day - she'd really believe it.

'Stay on the A38 for . . . 13 miles.'

'Oh shut up, arse face!' Caro grunted, wiping Bert's windscreen with the back of her hand as it started to mist up again. It was sodding freezing out there tonight, and now that she'd left the sprawl of Plymouth behind her, it was seriously dark.

Her parents had tried to talk her into staying at home tonight, suggesting that she should travel over in the morning when it was light, but Caro had been adamant. Christmas Eve was *not* the day to be driving anywhere. And anyway, she'd fought long and hard for a longer break from the shop this Christmas - Christmas Eve *and* Boxing Day off when you worked in retail was as rare as hen's teeth. She'd only been given it because of all the extra hours she'd been putting in and the fact that she had several weeks of annual leave that she had to squeeze in before March.

Besides, today was her birthday - and she didn't fancy finishing it up alone in her cold, grey flat.

She couldn't wait to get to her parents' house. She was planning on changing directly into her new tartan flannel pjs, getting her slippers on and cracking open the Baileys.

Her parents did Christmas Day in style, and she couldn't wait to share it with them without a certain unpleasant ex around to ruin everything.

'GAH!' Caro grunted aloud. Why did thoughts of him have to encroach on everything? It had happened a year ago. A whole year. He wasn't important.

'DASHING THROUGH THE SNOOOOOW!' she screeched at the top of her lungs, taking her frustration out on a little old lady in a Smart Car by slamming her foot to the floor and whizzing past.

'Take the next exit onto the A385.'

'I know, I know,' sighed Caro, glad to escape the busy dual carriageway onto the smaller roads that wound through the Devon countryside. It might not be that far from Plymouth to her parents' place, but it always took a lot longer to get there than she expected courtesy of the narrow, winding roads that were the specialty of South Devon.

Soon, Caro was navigating her way along a particularly dark stretch of road that she didn't recognise. She wasn't really that sure where she was, but that wasn't unusual. Suddenly, she caught the red flare of brake lights up ahead - a whole line-up of them. Oh great, seems she'd hit traffic.

Pulling to a stop at the back of the queue, she tapped the steering wheel irritably in time to the music, craning her neck and trying to see what the holdup was. There was nothing to see other than a long line of stationary cars.

After about ten minutes, Bert had started to steam up again and Caro's irritability level was reaching boiling point. It wasn't as though she was in a massive hurry, but now that she was on her way and all things Christmassy were awaiting her at the other end, she was desperate to get there and get started!

At long last things started to move - but not in the direction she'd been hoping for. The vehicle two cars up from her edged out of the queue and, after a pretty skilful three-point turn, headed back in the opposite direction. Then the car directly in front of her did the same.

Caro's heart started to hammer. She hated any kind of change in plans - especially when it came to driving or directions. But maybe the people in front of her knew something she didn't - maybe they'd managed to tune into some local travel news or something. Poor old Bert didn't even have a stereo, let alone the ability to feed her up-to-the minute travel info. The Google lady hadn't said a word to her since she'd hit the traffic. Typical.

There was a honk from the car behind and Caro swore in response. Yes, there was now the space of two cars in front of her. No, it wouldn't make a blind bit of difference to the idiot behind her if she pulled forward. The queue ahead was still completely stationary apart from the occasional car doing a U-turn.

'Oh, sod it!' Caro grunted. Peering over her shoulder and carefully down the other lane in case anyone was doing anything stupid, she indicated and swung the wheel around hard to the right. She pulled out as far as she could and then slammed the car back into reverse. After a rather ungainly six-and-a-half-point turn, she let out a whoop as she started to head away from the queue, back the way she'd come.

'Bollocks,' she then said quietly to no one in particular. What the hell was she supposed to do now? Her parents were expecting her.

'Make a U-turn,' said the cool voice of the Google lady.

'No, dumbass,' growled Caro, as she passed a tiny lane leading off to her left.

Maybe she should just go home, call her parents and head back over to them in the morning like they'd suggested. There must have been some kind of accident back there.

'In a quarter of a mile, take the next left.'

Caro raised her eyebrows. Next left? She'd never had to use an alternative route to her parents' before, but there were so many little lanes crisscrossing the county, it wasn't really a surprise that the idiot Satnav wanted to take her on a magical mystery tour. To follow or not to follow? That was the question.

'Take the next turning on the left.'

'Erm...'

'Turn left.'

'Oh, okay, okay you miserable old bat!'

Caro indicated, slowed right down and swung Bert carefully onto the narrowest country lane she'd ever driven down.

'Stay on this road for a quarter of a mile.'

'Fine!' Caro snapped, using the back of her hand to wipe at the foggy windscreen. She prayed that she didn't meet a car - or worse, a tractor - coming the other way. There was literally nowhere to go.

Away from the main road, it was even darker. Caro took the road slowly, her knuckles turning white as she gripped the wheel. After a few minutes - where the lane seemed to get even narrower, the high, leafless hedges squeezing tight on both sides of the little car - she passed a village sign for Little Bamton. At least it was somewhere she'd heard of before. She was sure she'd heard her parents talking about the pub here.

She came to a junction made up of two hump-back bridges - one leading away to the left, the other to the right.

'Come on then!' she sighed, waiting for the voice from her phone to give her the next instruction.

Nothing. She checked her rear-view mirror, but everything was completely dark, so she chanced a quick glance at her phone screen.

Connection lost

'Bloody great! Thanks so much!' shouted Caro.

HONK!

She jumped as lights flashed, and suddenly there was a car right up her behind.

'Really?!'

She had no idea which way she was meant to turn, but the angry dickhead behind her was indicating left, so Caro hastily indicated right and put her foot down, screeching away from them as fast as she could.

It didn't take long before she was passing through the picturesque heart of the village. Caro took a deep breath and slowed right down to peer at the chocolate-box cottages with their thatched roofs. This place was absolutely gorgeous. Gorgeous, but not particularly festive - there wasn't a Christmas light in sight.

Unfortunately, it also seemed to be completely lacking in any kind of road signs. Caro continued on through the village until she spotted a turning to her right that led straight up a steep hill. Why not? She'd give it a try. Maybe if she got up onto higher ground her Satnav would be able to kick back in.

She put her foot down and the little car made an angry roaring sound as it struggled against the steep slope.

'Come on, come on, come on!' she chanted, urging the old rust-bucket on. She pushed her foot a bit closer to the floor and Bert heaved his way up the steep, dark lane.

Suddenly, she crested the top of the hill. Caro wasn't fast enough to react, and she careened onto the flat, hitting the brakes for all she was worth. The entire world started to spin. She'd must have hit a patch of ice. Then the brakes locked, sending her into a violent spin on the narrow lane.

'No! Nooooooo!' Caro squealed, holding on for dear life as she smashed through the undergrowth on the verge. The whole car jerked ominously and with a crunching, crashing sound, she slipped sideways into a concealed ditch.

'Shit. Shitshitshit!' breathed Caro, her heart hammering in fright at finding herself sitting at a forty-five-degree angle.

She wasn't hurt - that had to be a good thing - but there was no hope in hell that she was going to be able to drive out of this mess.

Where was her phone? She focused in on the tinny sound of Michael Bublé crooning from somewhere behind her. She un-clicked her seatbelt and hunted around trying to reach the handset, just as a calm, cool voice interrupted the music.

'Please make a U-turn.'

CHAPTER 2

'Help!'

Caro knew in her heart that shouting was a pretty pointless exercise. It was pitch-dark outside, and no one was likely to be passing on foot given that this lane was in the arse-end of nowhere. Even if they did, would they be able to spot her little car stranded on its side in a ditch?

Okay, so she might be exaggerating slightly in her panic. Poor old Bert wasn't completely on his side - but he was at enough of an angle that meant the driver's door wouldn't open as it was window-side down into the mud, and the passenger door was at too much of an angle for her to be able to force it open long enough to scramble out without it slamming on her.

She'd just about managed to get the dodgy interior light to stay on in spite of the stuck switch and iffy wiring, then she'd wound down the passenger window and had started to bellow. Pointless. Completely pointless.

She was getting cold, and to make matters worse, the frigging Christmas music was still mocking her from somewhere behind her seat. She couldn't reach it no matter how hard she tried.

'Think, Caro!' she whispered, forcing herself to take long, calming breaths while she weighed up the facts. She was cold. She was stuck in a ditch in the middle of nowhere. She couldn't get out of the car, and she couldn't reach her phone.

'HELP!' It was the only viable reaction given the circumstances.

Okay, okay, this was ridiculous. She simply *had* to reach that phone. She couldn't stay in this ditch all night.

Caro leaned precariously sideways and wriggled her top-half through the gap between the two front seats. It had to be here somewhere!

She shifted her over-night bag out of the way from where it had toppled onto the floor, and then pulled out a handful of random rubbish from under the seat.

From her awkward position, she felt around blindly, wincing in disgust as her hand made contact with various unidentified bits of grit and sticky something-or-other. Her mum was right - she really ought to clean out her car more often. This was gross.

'Hello?!'

A sharp bang on the side of the car made Caro

jump. She let out a squeal as she felt herself wedge more firmly between the seats, bum in the air and head down.

'Hello?! Are you okay?' the gruff voice was coming from the direction of the open passenger window.

'I'm . . .' She wanted to say that she was fine, but that couldn't be further from the truth. 'I'm stuck!' she called back, her voice muffled.

'Okay - I'm coming in!' said the mystery voice. 'Hold on.'

Like she could do anything else!

Caro heard scrabbling noises from outside, and then the unmistakable sound of the car door being yanked open.

'Are you hurt?'

The voice was much closer now - deep and concerned - and the harsh light of some kind of torch flashed over the back seat.

'Nope. Just wedged,' she answered. She could feel herself going red, but she wasn't sure if it was due to being found bottom-side-up in a car in a ditch, or if it was just down to the fact that all her blood was starting to rush to her head.

'Okay . . . erm . . . if you make sure your hands are nowhere near the hinge-y bits, I'll swing the seat forward and see if that gives you a bit more room to move?'

Caro shifted her hands up out of the way, finally giving up any idea of getting hold of her phone. She could do without losing a finger on top of everything else.

'Clear,' she said, sounding like an extra from a medical drama.

There was a click and then the blessed relief of a bit more wiggle-room as the seat shifted on its runners and hinged forward.

Caro struggled backwards into the driver's seat, pushed her hair out of her face and grinned sheepishly at the shadowy figure who was hanging precariously through the open doorway.

'I'm Sam.'

'Caro,' she puffed, trying to get her breath back.

'Okay Caro, take my hand - let's get you out of there!' he said.

'My phone's disappeared onto the floor back there somewhere,' she said.

'Leave everything for now - it's more important that you're safe!'

Caro shifted unsteadily uphill into the passenger seat, grabbing her handbag off the floor as she went. She slung it securely across her body, reached out to grab hold of the stranger's free hand, and began to mountain-climb her way out of the little car.

Sam held her steady with one hand while making sure the door didn't slam shut on them both with the other.

Eventually, with much huffing and puffing, she made it out into the cold night air. It took her a few moments to find her feet in the deep, tussocky grass that lined the bank.

Sam let the door of the car slam closed and, turning to join her, offered her a steady arm as they clambered their way back towards the slippery country lane.

'What happened?' he asked, concern just about visible on his face in the pale light coming from his phone. He was tall and had a mop of dark, floppy hair, but that was about all she could make out.

Caro shrugged. 'I'm not sure - everything happened so fast. I came to the top of the hill, and then before I knew it, poor old Bert was spinning and then we were both sitting at a funny angle in the ditch!'

She looked at her car again and a little shiver ran down her spine. That could have been so much worse.

'You must have hit a patch of ice,' he said, shaking his head. 'These back lanes are always the last to be gritted.'

'I guess so. I wasn't going very fast, thank goodness. I don't know the road. My stupid Satnav brought me into the village when there was a snarl-up on the main road and then promptly stopped working, so I was going extra careful.'

'Good thing too.'

'Thank heavens you found me,' she smiled gratefully at him.

'You'd have got yourself out eventually.'

'Yeah, I guess so,' she said, shrugging and rubbing her arms. In reality, she knew that there was no way she'd have managed to get herself out of the car without help.

'You sure you're not hurt?' he asked.

'I'm fine - really,' she assured him. 'Just wondering how the hell I'm going to get poor old Bert out of there.

'Bert?'

'The car. And it's a perfectly good name!'

'Oh - yes of course,' he said, a slight snort escaping him. 'Well, I reckon your best bet is to ask Lyndon for help. He's one of the local farmers. He could probably bring his tractor up and tow you out of there.'

'Great!' she said. 'That would be fantastic. But - my phone's in the car and-'

Sam was shaking his head. 'There's no way he'd be able to do it tonight. Lyndon will be down at the pub. Trust me, you don't want him near poor old Bert at this point - he'll be at least a couple of pints into his evening by now.'

'Oh. Great.' Caro sighed. 'Sam, can I borrow your phone? I'm due at my parents' any minute and they're going to be worried!'

Sam shook his head. 'There's no signal up here. Look, it's probably best if you come back to my place. You can use the landline.'

Caro paused a moment. Go back to this random man's house . . . in the middle of nowhere? What was he doing out on a dark lane at this time of night anyway?'

'Don't look so worried!' he huffed, clearly catching

the concern as it flashed across her face. 'I swear I'm completely safe. Look - my place is just over there.' He pointed at a cluster of twinkling lights just up the road. 'I was going to head down to the pub, but I changed my mind - it's going to start snowing any minute. So I was just about to pop the Land Rover back in the barn when I heard a crash and came to investigate - nothing more sinister than that.'

'If you're sure?' said Caro. She was now cold to the core and hugging herself wasn't offering much comfort.

'I don't think you've got much choice, to be honest!' said Sam, holding out his hands to catch the first few snowflakes as they fluttered down around them.

'Snow!' said Caro.

'Yep, told you! Come on - let's get inside and warm up a bit. We'll call your parents, and you can make a plan. Maybe you can get a taxi over to them tonight, or get them to pick you up, and then come back to sort out your car in the morning?'

Caro paused for just a second before nodding. 'Okay, thanks.'

'Alright - let's go!'

They'd only taken about a dozen strides along the lane before Caro's feet nearly went out from underneath her and she did an excellent windmill impression as she tried to keep herself upright. The only thing that saved her from hitting the road was Sam's hand as it wrapped tightly around her arm, steadying her just in time.

'Crap!' she squeaked, clutching at his arm while her feet continued to slide even though she wasn't moving a muscle.

'Indeed,' he grunted.

'I can't move!'

'Yes you can! You're literally just one step away from me, and there's no ice here.'

Caro looked down at her feet, willing herself to take a step.

'Not a fan of ice-skating?'

She let out another little squeak, and Sam sighed.

'Hold on!' He shoved his phone in a pocket, took a firm grip of both her hands and pulled her towards him, off the patch of ice. 'Okay - you're safe!'

Caro was suddenly thankful that it was so dark - she could tell by the heat radiating from her face that she was doing an excellent cranberry impression right now.

'Thanks. Sorry. I'm a complete coward!'

'Look - if we stick to the grass verge as much as we can, we won't hit any more.'

Sam dropped her hands and picked his way back to the edge of the lane. Caro didn't move a muscle.

'Coming?'

She nodded but still didn't move.

Without saying another word, Sam went back to her side and offered her his arm. Caro took it gratefully and, with her legs shaking, let him lead her to safety.

Sure, she was a strong, independent woman, but right now, she was a strong, independent woman who would prefer not to land on her backside.

CHAPTER 3

By the time Sam led her off the road into a yard, the snow had set in properly and was coming down thick and fast. The magical flurries were illuminated by golden light spilling from an absolutely stunning cabin ahead of them. It was like nothing she'd ever seen before, and she stopped dead to stare at it.

There, in front of her, stood a giant, double-storey triangular structure - the front of which was made of wood and glass. It was too dark to see any details of the sloping sides, but there was an impressive woodpile stacked under the raised deck that ran right the way across the front of the triangle, and she could just make out a chimney poking through the sloping left hand side of the roof. Sniffing the cold air, she caught the whiff of wood smoke and was suddenly desperate to get into the warmth.

Aware that she was gawping, Caro quickly pulled herself together and followed Sam around to the right of the cabin, picking her way gingerly along the dim path.

Sam stepped under a small porch that interrupted the slope of the roof. Caro followed, grateful to step out of the snow that was swirling around them with enthusiasm and already starting to settle.

Glad to be on dry, non-slippery ground, Caro stamped her feet to get rid of the worst of slush that had already built up and ruffled her hair in an attempt to dislodge the damp flakes that were clinging to the ebony strands. She waited, shivering slightly as Sam fitted his key into the lock.

'Come on in,' he said, pushing the door open.

As soon as she closed the door behind her, warmth seemed to flood into her bones, and she let out a sigh of relief.

Following Sam's lead, she kicked off her damp shoes and nudged them under a low table that stood a few paces inside the wood-lined hallway.

'Here, give me your jacket and I'll put it in front of the wood-burner to dry,' said Sam. He held out his hand and waited while she struggled to peel it off - her numb fingers not making things easy. As soon as she handed it over, he disappeared down the hall and through a doorway to the left without a word. Caro padded along behind him in her socks.

She stopped in the doorway and stared in awe at the gorgeous room in front of her. She didn't know what she'd been expecting after seeing the front of the cabin, but it certainly wasn't this. The room was at the base of the triangle. The sloping walls were made of a honey-coloured wood that made the space feel incredibly warm and cosy.

There were two squashy sofas with snuggly-looking throws over the back of them, a low coffee table in between. One entire wall was made of glass and wood and was obviously the front of the cabin she'd been admiring just now, its wide, glass double door led out onto the deck, and she could imagine it was a beautiful place to sit in the summer. Right now, the wall of windows was filled with swirling, drifting snow.

'Come in, come in! Have a seat a sec,' said Sam as he arranged her coat on the back of a wooden chair. He dragged it over to stand in front of a spectacular wood-burner that looked like it was hovering, unsupported, above a circular stone hearth.

Caro smiled at him and moved to perch on one of the sofas. It was like sitting on a cloud, and a sudden wave of exhaustion flooded through her. All she wanted to do was tuck her feet up under her, snuggle back into the cushions and close her eyes. She watched as Sam added a log to the fire then looked around the cosy room, willing her eyes not to drift closed.

The wall that separated this room from the hallway

had been built so that the entire thing formed a gigantic bookcase - and it was full-to-bursting. She longed to take a closer look but couldn't muster the energy to stand back up.

No. She mustn't make herself too comfortable. She needed to call her parents and sort out getting to their place before this snow got any worse.

'Sam, sorry to be a pain - but can I use your phone? The weather's just getting worse out there, and my parents will be freaking out!'

'Of course, here,' he went over to a desk tucked away behind a wrought-iron spiral staircase that presumably led to the room upstairs, grabbed the handset and tossed it over onto the cushions next to her. 'Take your time. I'll make us a drink - tea? Something stronger?'

'Tea would be amazing - thank you! Black, no sugar?'

He raised his eyebrows. 'Coming up!' he said, turning to head out of the room.

'Sam?'

He turned back to her.

'Erm . . . where are we? I mean - for someone to give me a lift!'

'Blackbird Barn,' he said. Then he grabbed a pad and pen from the coffee table, jotted down the details for her, handed them over and disappeared without another word.

Caro quickly dialled her parents' number and settled back further on the sofa as she waited for one of them to pick up.

'Mum?'

'Oh thank goodness! Caro!'

Her mum's voice quavered down the line at her and Caro smiled - suddenly everything felt like it was going to be okay again. Her mum always managed to have that effect on her.

'GERALD!'

Caro hastily pulled the receiver away from her ear before her mum managed to burst her eardrum.

'GERALD - CARO'S OKAY!'

She could hear her dad muttering something in the background.

'Mum? Of course I'm okay! Why, what's happened?'

'What do you mean *of course* - where are you? Haven't you heard?'

'Heard what?'

'About the massive accident?' said her mum.

'Accident? Is that why the road was blocked?'

'You saw it?' her mum demanded. 'Gerald - she saw it!'

'I didn't see it - I just hit traffic.'

'Caro! You're not meant to be on the phone when you're driving! Hang up immediately!!'

'Mum - slow down, it's okay, I'm not driving at the moment.'

'Oh. Why not?'

Caro took a deep, calming breath. 'I hit traffic - sat there for about ten minutes and then all the cars around me started to turn around - so I did too. I was using my Satnav and it suggested a different route - through Little Bamton? So I took that.'

'So why have you stopped? Will you be here soon?'

'Well, eh, no. Sorry mum - that's why I'm calling. I'm fine - but I *did* have a little accident.'

'Oh no! Gerald, she had an accident!'

'It was quite icy - and I skidded into a ditch.'

Her mum let out a squeak, and Caro felt bad for scaring her.

'It's okay mum, a local guy helped me out and brought me back to his place so I could call you.'

'Why didn't you just use your mobile.'

'Erm… well, that's lodged somewhere in the car. And the car is still in the ditch.'

'Oh Caro - and on your birthday too. You sure you're okay?'

'Really mum - I'm fine. I'm just having a cup of tea. I was going to ask if you could come and get me, but it's snowing really badly here.'

'Yes - it's just started here too,' said her mum, 'and I'm afraid we've both had a little tipple already.'

Caro's heart sank.

'I'll see if I can get a taxi and I'll call you back to let you know.'

'I don't think that's a good idea love.'

'What do you mean?'

'Well - that accident has completely closed the main road - it was a serious one by all accounts. And from what you're saying, the back roads are too dangerous. I expect they'll be out gritting and clearing tonight, so it should be safer by the morning.'

'But . . .'

'No, Caro - I don't want you risking it. Your dad can come and get you tomorrow if your car needs some work.'

'But mum, I'm in the middle of nowhere in a stranger's house!'

'I thought you said that you were in a village?'

'Little Bamton.'

'Ooh Gerald - she's in Little Bamton!'

'I'm quite a way outside the village-'

Caro rolled her eyes as her dad said something indistinct on the other end.

'Well, there's a lovely pub there,' said her mum, 'I'm sure they've got rooms. Maybe your stranger could walk you down to the village?'

'Maybe...' said Caro, trailing off as she heard her dad muttering something else.

She sighed. Caro knew for certain that there was no way she was going to take her chances and skate all the way back down to the village - it had been difficult enough getting this far. But, if she was going to have to camp on Sam's sofa for the night, she didn't want her mum worrying any more than she already was.

'Mum - I need to go and sort this out!' she prompted gently, knowing that these three-way chats with her parents could go on forever if she wasn't careful.

'Of course love. Your dad was just saying that the son of one of his metal detecting cronies lives in Little Bamton. Tragic story, actually. He was just trying to remember his first name. Surname is Wills.'

'Oh. Erm - that's . . . nice?' Caro smiled to herself. If she'd found herself on Mars, she was certain her parents would know someone who lived in the same crater where she'd crash-landed. Somehow, they knew everyone.

'Okay love. You go and sort yourself out.'

'Thanks mum. And don't worry - I'm fine. I'll see you tomorrow!'

'Yes - we'll wait to hear from you.'

'Don't forget I don't have my mobile! Let me give you the landline here and the address - just so you have it.'

Caro quickly read the details off the little slip of paper Sam had handed her.

'Love you, mum!'

'You too, love - happy birthday.'

Caro hung up and sighed again. This wasn't quite the way she'd planned to spend her birthday.

'You done?' Sam appeared in the doorway carrying two mugs. He'd clearly been waiting for her to finish on the phone.

'Yeah - thanks,' she said, gratefully taking a large mug from him and cradling it to her. 'Bad news I'm afraid.'

Sam nodded, sitting on the sofa opposite her. 'I just looked online - the main road is still closed. Looks like you just missed a really bad accident there.'

'That's what mum said. And both of them have had a drink so they can't come to my rescue.'

'I'm not sure that would have been a very good plan anyway - have you seen it out there?' he asked, pointing towards the thick glass double-doors.

Caro turned. The snow was still coming down in flurries, but as she popped her cup down on the low table and headed over to take a better look, she gasped. In the twenty minutes since they'd come inside, everything outside had turned white - and it didn't look like it was thinking about stopping any time soon.

'I think you'd better stay,' said Sam.

Caro turned to look at him. 'Are you sure? I could see if a taxi would come out?'

Sam shook his head. 'No point anyone risking their necks if they don't have to.'

'No. You're right. Thank you,' she said, feeling bad for ruining his evening.

'No problem.'

Caro padded back to the sofa and sat back down. 'Oh crap - my bag is still in the back of Bert.'

'We'll get it in the morning - I can lend you some things.'

She nodded gratefully and sighed.

'Cheer up - it could have been so much worse. You're safe - and I'm sure Lyndon will get Bert out of the ditch in the morning.'

Caro forced a smile. She knew he was trying to be nice, but this really, *really* wasn't how she'd planned to spend her hard-earned time off. She felt like she wanted to stamp her foot.

'What a bloody brilliant birthday this is turning out to be!' she muttered.

'It's your birthday?' Sam asked in surprise.

She nodded glumly. 'Yep.'

'Oh.' He got to his feet and disappeared back out into the hallway.

What a strange bloke.

'*Happy birthday,*' she muttered under her breath. She stared grumpily around her, realising for the first time what was missing from this beautiful room. There wasn't a single Christmas decoration to be seen - except for a large tree over near the double doors - which was completely bare.

Caro got to her feet and wandered over towards it. On the floor, right next to it, was a storage box. Its lid was off and she could see that it was full to the brim with decorations. It looked like Sam had been interrupted just as he'd been about to start decorating . . . he was leaving it a little bit late, wasn't he?

She had just crouched down to examine a vintage glass and gold bauble that was resting on the top of the pile when the sound of Sam clearing his throat behind her made her jump back up. She spun around guiltily only to find him standing in the doorway with a plate in his hand bearing a chunk of fruit cake, a flickering birthday candle poking out of the top.

'Please don't make me sing,' he grumbled, his face deadly serious.

'What's all this?' said Caro in surprise.

'You said it's your birthday - this is the last piece of cake I've got left. But . . . well, birthdays should be special. . .' he trailed off.

'Wow, erm, thanks!' she said, heading back over towards Sam.

He held the plate out towards her and leaning forwards ever so slightly, she blew out the candle.

'Make a wish!'

'Sing?' she grinned at him.

Sam sighed, and then, much to her surprise, he opened his mouth and started to sing *happy birthday*, sounding a little bit like an angry bumblebee.

'Sorry,' he said once he'd finished, turning pink. 'Singing's not my strong suit!'

'You were perfect,' she couldn't wipe the gleeful smile from her face. 'Thank you.'

Sam shrugged. 'Eat the cake. It's good, I promise. Lucy down at the pub made it for me, and she's a baking genius. Then I'll show you to your room.'

Her room? She didn't have to sleep on the sofa? She

plucked the candle out of the slice of cake and took a huge bite.

Sam finally cracked a smile, and his entire face seemed to light up. YUM! Maybe her birthday wasn't so bad after all.

CHAPTER 4

Caro woke to a bright, opaline glow. She peered around her, blinking groggily at her unfamiliar surroundings. Why was it so light already? Surely it was first thing in the morning in the middle of winter? She shuffled her way up the huge bed and, sitting back against the mound of pillows, she was faced with a truly stunning view.

The room Sam had shown her to the previous evening was the one at the top of the tightly-wound wrought-iron staircase. It was directly above the sitting room at the top of the triangular cabin. The ceiling sloped from the ridge above her and ran right down to the floor on either side of the room - the effect was a bit like sleeping in a very large, wooden tent.

Best of all was the wall at the front of the room - a large triangular panel made almost entirely of glass.

Caro scrambled out of the pile of soft, fluffy pillows and made her way over to take a better look.

Well, that explained the light. The entire world had turned white over night. The snow had carpeted the ground and was still falling. There must be several feet of it lying in the yard, and as she peered over towards the road, all she could see was more white. Ah crap.

Caro sighed. Sure, it was beautiful, but somehow she couldn't imagine it was going to be possible to haul poor old Bert out of the ditch in this, let alone get to her parents' house. Her heart sank.

Just then, Sam appeared around the corner of the cabin below her, bobble hat and thick jacket firmly in place as he strode over towards one of the barns she'd glimpsed the night before.

Caro smiled as she watched him. Sure, he'd been a bit grumpy and definitely a man of few words, but it wasn't as though she could really blame him - she had, quite literally, crashed his Christmas plans after all.

Sam turned towards the cabin and Caro hastily drew away from the huge window, not wanting him to see her in her full, just-out-of-bed glory. It was a bit much for him to see her in her PJs the day after they'd met!

Actually, scratch that. These weren't even her pyjamas, were they?! She'd had to ask him last night if she could borrow a pair as all her stuff was still in the ditch with Bert. Oh, the horror!

Caro looked down and smoothed the front of the

red tartan, flannel top he'd handed her with the matching bottoms. They were way too big for her, but they were also way cuter than she'd expected.

Gah - she'd have to get dressed in yesterday's clothes, wouldn't she? Unless there was any chance they could salvage her bag from Bert's back seat. Somehow, that seemed pretty unlikely, what with the extra layer of snow that was bound to be blanketing him by now.

Well, there was nothing for it. Yesterday's clothes it had to be. But there was no way she was changing in here - what if Sam walked past again? It wasn't as though there was any privacy what with an entire wall made of glass and no curtains!

Caro quickly gathered her clothes together and headed out into the hallway. Directly opposite her door was another, presumably leading to Sam's bedroom. It was cracked open, and the temptation to stick her head in and see what kind of man-cave he had going on in there was massive, but after a quick mental telling-off for being so nosy, she managed to talk herself out of it. Sam had been nothing but kind to her - he didn't deserve her snooping into his private space.

She had to admit she was surprised that he used the room at the back of the cabin, leaving the bedroom at the front - clearly designed to be the master bedroom - empty. Whatever, it wasn't any of her business. Maybe he just preferred the relative privacy of not having an entire glass wall looking out over the yard to wake up to every morning.

She turned away and headed into the little bathroom that filled the far end of the hallway. There wasn't much she could do other than splash water on her face, rake her hands through her tangled mop and grimace as she pulled on yesterday's pants. She *had* to break in to Bert.

As soon as she was done, she went back to her bedroom, quickly made the bed, folded her borrowed PJs and then headed down the little spiral staircase into the sitting room.

The wood-burner was already roaring in the corner, and the room felt welcoming and cosy, even though she felt like she could reach out and touch the blanket of snow through the incredible glass wall.

Sam must still be outside somewhere, so she padded across the room towards the downstairs hallway in search of the kitchen. She headed down the hall, rounding the gap at the far end, and gasped. She'd found the kitchen, and breakfast was already laid out on the table for her.

She stepped towards the scrubbed, farmhouse-style table and her eye was caught by a sheet of lined paper with her name scrawled across the top of it.

Caro,

Hope you slept well. Am out in the yard sorting a few

things out and checking my workshop is okay after the snow. I've made waffles- hope that's okay for you! They're in the bottom of the Aga to keep warm. If not- there's cereal, eggs, toast, fruit, yogurt- whatever you fancy- just help yourself.

Sam x

Caro ran her finger over his name and the kiss at the end, and smiled. Then she gave herself a little shake, told herself to pull it together, and went in search of the waffles. Okay for her? She should say so!

Her attention was briefly caught by a second spiral staircase - a mirror of the one in the sitting room. This one must lead up into Sam's bedroom. She stared up at the opening in the ceiling for a moment, and then turned her attention back to the important task of stuffing her face.

After piling her plate high with chopped fruit, fresh waffles and a generous drizzle of syrup, Caro sat down and sighed. Well - this was the last way she'd expected to start her Christmas Eve, but as the scent of the warm waffles and freshly poured coffee drifted up to meet her, she had to admit - it wasn't a bad way to start the day.

Taking a bite, she smiled as she remembered the birthday cake from the night before and just how special Sam's off-key rendition of *Happy Birthday* had made her feel. Suddenly it wasn't just the first taste of her delicious breakfast that was making her feel all warm inside.

Setting down her fork, Caro reached over and picked up Sam's note again. She hastily folded it and popped it into her pocket.

❄

Sam still hadn't returned by the time she'd finished eating. She'd downed a second cup of coffee and even done the washing up, but there was no sign of him anywhere. After popping various dishes back into the fridge so that they wouldn't spoil, Caro went in search of her jacket. She found it hanging on a peg in the hallway - perfectly warm and dry after a night in front of the wood-burner. She buttoned it up and quickly pulled her shoes on, keen now to get outside and find out what Sam was up to.

Cracking open the door, a blast of cold air hit her full in the face, and she quickly stepped outside and closed it to stop all the heat escaping.

Sam had been busy while she'd been luxuriating over her long, lazy breakfast. He'd cleared the snow from the path to the front of the cabin. Caro could see that it was even deeper than she'd thought - at least three feet in some places. It had pretty-much stopped falling for the moment - just a fine sprinkling of glittering crystals drifted down from the pearly sky.

She made her way carefully along the cleared

pathway to the yard at the front of the cabin, to find that Sam had scraped a wide swathe of snow away from the open-fronted barn all the way to the gateway that opened onto the road.

In the middle of the yard stood an old Land Rover, its engine running, the exhaust fumes pluming in the freezing morning air. Caro tugged her jacket even tighter around her and shivered slightly. She still couldn't see Sam anywhere.

She picked her way across the yard to take a look inside the barn, but it was completely empty other than tidy racks of tools stacked along each wall. The centre was clearly reserved for keeping the Land Rover warm and dry.

Sighing, Caro turned and followed another carefully cleared pathway around the back of the cabin towards another wooden shed. This one was like the cabin itself in miniature - it looked like it was only one storey high and instead of gleaming glass windows, the front triangle was taken up by a large wooden double doorway.

One of the doors was standing partially open, so she peered through the gap and spotted Sam, his head bent low over a large sheaf of papers that were laid out on a bench to one side of the space.

'Hey,' she said quietly, not wanting to make him jump.

Sam jumped anyway, his head whipping around. 'Oh - Caro - hi! Sorry, I didn't see you there.'

Caro smiled at him, feeling suddenly shy and more like she was intruding on this stranger's life than ever before.

'Thanks for breakfast,' she said.

'No problem.' He continued to look at her but didn't say anything else. Caro shifted her weight uncomfortably, not sure what to say next.

'So... erm... it snowed a bit then!'

'Yup.'

Great. So, he was really going to make her do all the work here, wasn't he. The warm, snuggly feelings that had body-snatched her over breakfast were quickly becoming a distant memory.

'So ... erm ... do you think Lyndon might be able to rescue Bert today?'

Sam shook his head. 'I called him earlier. There's no way he'll be able to do it until they clear the road. It's completely white. He might be able to get the tractor over here, but he wouldn't be able to tow Bert out with it being this slippery.'

'Oh. Right.'

'Look - I've got the Land Rover out. Grab your stuff and we'll head down to the village. I'm sure we'll either be able to get you a lift to your parents' place or a taxi or something.'

Caro's heart sank. 'You think you should drive in this?'

'Don't have much choice, do I?' he grunted, turning

back to the plans on his bench. 'Meet you by the Land Rover in a minute.'

Caro turned her back on him quickly so that he didn't see the look of hurt that flashed across her face. She knew she'd been a royal pain-in-the-bum for the guy, but she really hadn't meant to put him out. He sounded really pissed-off, and it felt like a bit of a slap in the face after that gorgeous breakfast.

Never mind. By the sound of it, she'd be out of his hair before she knew it and would finally be able to settle into the cosy Christmas she'd had planned with her family. Sam and his beautiful, strange home would quickly become nothing more than a story to tell over the sherry.

CHAPTER 5

Caro clambered into the icy interior of the Land Rover and plonked her handbag on her lap. In reality, that's all she'd had to go back into the cabin to collect, but she'd taken a few minutes to make sure she'd left the bedroom as pristine as she'd found it.

Descending the tight spiral staircase into the sitting room, she'd taken one last, long look around the space, her eyes catching once more on the bare tree with its box of ornaments sitting at the ready. She wondered if Sam would ever get around to decorating it, and guessed she'd never actually find out.

Then she'd made sure she'd completely tidied up the breakfast things before heading back out into the snow. It was the least she could do.

She probably hadn't been more than a few minutes, but as she settled onto the uncomfortable seat next to

Sam, he let out an impatient sigh as though he'd been waiting for her for hours.

Caro grit her teeth and pulled her jacket tighter around herself. Moody git! She took in a deep, calming breath, and tried not to let out a squeak of fear as Sam gunned the old vehicle forwards and its tyres skidded slightly on the slippery surface of the newly-cleared yard.

'You sure we should be driving? I could always walk down to the village?' she said nervously.

'You - walk in this? I wouldn't dream of making you do that after seeing you on the ice last night,' he said. 'Besides - this old thing has four-wheel-drive - we should get down there fine. Anyway, it's mostly down-hill - we can slide most of the way if we have to!' he deadpanned.

Caro gripped the strap of her handbag tighter and swallowed.

'I was joking,' Sam grunted, peeping at her side-ways. 'I might not manage to drive back up, but that's okay - I can always leave it in the pub car park and walk. Lucy won't mind.'

Sam pulled out onto the little road - which hadn't been cleared at all and was still a virgin blanket of snow - clearly no one had been idiot enough to drive this way yet.

By the time they slid to a halt at the junction at the bottom of the hill, Caro's knuckles were white and even Sam was looking tense, his shoulders up around his ears and his jaw set in a firm line. They hadn't spoken a word as they'd slalomed down the hill, and it felt like a bit of a miracle that they'd made it this far in one piece. Caro had peered sadly at the white hump in the ditch that was Bert as they passed him. Sam had been right - there was no way he'd be able to be dragged out of there today - and it wasn't like anyone would be willing to do it tomorrow on Christmas day, was it?!

'Okay,' said Sam, the tension seeping into his voice as he turned carefully onto the main village road, 'you were right. Driving down was a bad, bad plan.'

Caro nodded fervently. 'Promise you won't drive back?' she said.

'That's an easy promise to make - I don't think I'd make it back up the hill even if I cared to try it.'

'Sam?'

'Yeah?'

'Thank you. For everything.'

Sam indicated and pulled carefully into a small white square that stood at the back of the thatched pub. Killing the engine, he turned to her.

'You're welcome.'

'I mean it - you've been really kind.'

'Yeah, well - it wasn't like you could kip in the car, was it?' he said.

Caro shrugged. She'd said her piece. Maybe it was best if she just got on with the next bit of her plan and sorted out a lift home. She just hoped that the main road was in a better state than the lanes - otherwise she was well and truly screwed.

'So, what's the plan?' she asked eventually, as Sam just sat there staring at the back of the pub. It was looking chocolate-box perfect with its cap of pure white snow, its chimney already wreathed in tendrils of wood smoke.

He shook his head, coming out of some kind of daydream. 'Erm - I need to quickly head over to the craft centre - just to check everything is in one piece after the snow, then-'

'Ooh, craft centre? Do you work there?' Caro interrupted. She loved crafts - especially anything to do with textiles and up-cycling.

'Not exactly - I've got a unit there, and we all keep an eye out for each other. I doubt any of the others have been able to get here to check it over yet.'

'What do you do?' she asked, cursing herself silently. How self-absorbed had she been last night that she hadn't asked him before now?!

'Why don't you come and take a look?' he said. 'Lucy might not have quite opened up the pub yet. The centre is just around the corner. We'll check it over, and then pop into the bar and get you a lift sorted?'

'Okay - thanks, I'd like that,' she said, surprised that he wasn't desperate to get her off his hands straight away.

Hopping down from her cold perch, Caro wished two things: that she had a warmer coat with her and that her shoes were more suited to traipsing around in the snow. As it was, her light jacket was doing a pathetic job of keeping the cold air out, and it wasn't helped by the fact that the snow was deep enough to spill up and over the top of her leather shoe-boots. They would be soaked through in just a few minutes.

Wrapping her arms around herself, she gingerly followed Sam out of the car park and around the front of the pub. He glanced back at her and came to an abrupt stop.

'You're cold!' he said, and without another word he took off his heavy wool coat and held it open for her.

'Oh, I can't!' she said in surprise. 'You'll freeze.'

'Only if you don't get a move on,' he grumbled.

Caro hesitated for another second before giving in and letting him help her slip her arms into the blissful warmth of the extra layer.

She eyed him, feeling guilty for leaving him standing there in just a jumper as his residual body-heat and the musky, sandalwood scent that clung to the coat wrapped themselves around her.

'Thank you,' she sighed.

'It's fine. I'm wearing two jumpers anyway!'

He led her across the little square away from the pub, and they ducked under a snow-covered willow arch, pausing to unlock a wrought-iron gate into what looked like a mews row.

'These used to be old stables,' he explained, as Caro stepped gratefully off the snow to walk along the dry pavement under the overhanging roofs of one side of little shops and studios.

'These are gorgeous!' she said, stopping to peer in through one of the windows. It was a small but perfectly formed artist's studio. The walls were completely covered with beautiful paintings depicting village life - and in the centre of the space was an easel on which stood a canvas - clearly a work-in-progress. Next to the easel was a little wooden cart, groaning under the weight of paint tubes, brushes, bottles and a huge palette that looked like it had at least an inch of paint layered onto it.

'That's Eve's place. She's an incredible painter - though you should see some of the charcoal sketches she does too!'

Caro moved on to the next window, full of willow wreaths set around a life-sized woven-willow reindeer.

'Okay, wow!'

Sam chuckled. 'You carry on looking around - I'm just going in here to check things over, okay?'

'Oh, okay,' Caro smiled at Sam, and watched as he unlocked one of the units a little further up on the opposite side. She desperately wanted to go over to his window and suss out what he had in there, but figuring she was already doing a good job of putting a spanner in the works of his quiet Christmas Eve plans, she snuggled down further into his coat and decided to check out more of the other shops before following him in.

The next one she came to was a bit of a let-down though. Clearly the little space had recently been vacated. There was a scattering of mail littering the mat just inside the door. Pressing her nose against the window, Caro peered in at the space. Other than what looked like a couple of empty jewellery cases and a table, it was completely bare.

A bubble of excitement formed in Caro's chest. If she wasn't much mistaken, this felt strangely similar to what she imagined love at first sight might feel like.

She craned her neck, trying to see every inch of the space. It looked perfect. In her mind's eye, she could see it filled with racks of perfectly chosen vintage finds. And over there, where that ugly table was, she could imagine her gorgeous old singer sewing machine, ready for her to make her one-off up-cycled bags and accessories. The window would be full of them, shown off in the most beautiful displays. She would change it every week. She'd be known for them . . .

She had to find out more! Abandoning her plan to give Sam a bit of peace and quiet, she marched straight over to his unit and popped her head around the open door.

The sight that met her eyes managed to do the impossible and make her forget her own excitement for just a second.

Sam's shop was full of the most beautiful pieces of hand-crafted wooden furniture she'd ever seen. Caro wandered up to a love-seat and, unable to stop herself, trailed her fingers along the dark, glossy seat. She marvelled at the way the grain came to life under the lights - making it look like it had been carved out of flowing water.

Caro tore her eyes away from its sinuous lines to look around her at the walls, all of which were covered in hand-drawn blue-prints for cabins very similar to Sam's own home. These were interspersed with arty shots of completed cabins - at sunset, beside a river, lights glimmering from behind a fine veil of snowflakes.

'What do you think?'

Sam's quiet voice made her jump. For a moment she'd completely forgotten he was in there with her.

'Stunning,' she said simply.

'Thanks!'

'I mean - you made all these?' she said, gesturing around at the furniture.

Sam nodded. 'Yep.'

'And the cabins?'

'Those are my *real* job, I guess,' he quirked an eyebrow. 'I sometimes use the studio as a meeting room for first-contact with clients, so it made sense to show off my work like this.'

'Right... and that would make the furniture...?'

'A hobby,' he said shortly.

'Wow!' Caro said simply. 'I wish I had a hobby that meant I ended up with something like this.' She ran her hand over a gorgeous little table that had caught her eye. Ooh she wanted it. It was honey-coloured, all sinuous, natural lines so that it looked like it had grown straight up out of the floor.

'Do you make them here?' she asked, struggling to tear her eyes away.

'Sometimes,' he said. 'Take a look.' He beckoned her towards a partition at the back of the studio space, and she followed him.

Where the front of his unit was all polished-to-perfection, this half was where the magic happened. It smelled of warm wood and beeswax. There were various bits of intimidating-looking machinery lined up around the edge of the space, and a large bench was set in the centre.

'I do a lot of the big work back at my workshop behind the cabin - that's where all the saws are - it would be a health and safety nightmare to have them here. But I do love working in here when I can. I open up these two doors so that people can watch from the shop, and sometimes I do demonstrations.'

'So cool!' enthused Caro. She wandered over towards one of the machines, 'So, ah, what's this torture device?'

Sam smiled. 'That's a lathe. I use it for turning legs, spindles . . . that kind of thing.'

Caro nodded, and then her eye caught on something standing on one of the shelves towards the back of the workshop. She headed straight over towards it and, without thinking, took it in her hands. She stroked her fingers along the partially-finished carving.

Half of it was still a roughly-cut block of wood. The other half was a meticulously-carved figure of half an angel.

'Oh wow, Sam, what's this?' she said, turning to him with the angel still in her hands.

Caro knew the moment she caught the look on his face that she'd done something terrible. The colour disappeared from his cheeks. His lips grew thin, like he was biting on them to stop something escaping, and she saw him swallow hard.

'I'm sorry . . .' she said, not really knowing what she was apologising for, but really and truly meaning it. She began to turn to replace the angel on the shelf.

'Put that back.' Sam's voice was low and shaking - with rage or sorrow or . . . some kind of emotion Caro couldn't pinpoint.

'Of course, I'm sorry.' She hastily slipped it back on the shelf, and then headed straight back towards the studio. 'I'll meet you outside,' she muttered as she passed him, but wasn't sure if he'd heard her - he was staring hard at the angel, eyes gleaming.

CHAPTER 6

Caro strode straight out of the front door of Sam's unit and decided to explore what other shops the little craft-centre held, but her heart wasn't in it anymore. Sure, she stopped and stared at each of the window displays, but she wasn't really seeing them. Instead she was trying to figure Sam out. One minute he was kind, warm - even funny. And then he was grumpy, angry, snapping at her. She knew it was her fault really - she shouldn't be so inquisitive.

She sighed and headed over for a last look at the empty unit. She hadn't asked Sam about it, and now she guessed she probably wouldn't get the chance. Ah well, it wasn't as though her pie-in-the-sky dreams could come true anyway. She had a job. She had a flat. And they were both back in Plymouth. She tore her eyes away from the empty shop only to find Sam standing a few feet away, looking at her awkwardly.

'I'm sorry,' he said in a low voice.

'No, I'm sorry!' she said quickly. 'I shouldn't have done that - it wasn't my place - just picking things up like that.'

'It's fine. Really.'

He didn't look fine. He might be saying the words but he was still frowning and Caro didn't feel like she was off the hook at all. She went to open her mouth to apologise again, but Sam beat her to it.

'That piece - well - it just reminds me of something I'd rather forget.'

'I get it,' she said in a tight voice. She didn't, not really. Why have it sitting there in full view if he'd rather forget about it? This man was a complete mystery.

'Okay,' said Sam. 'Well, everything looks like it's in one piece here. Let's go get you on your way.'

'Sounds like a plan,' she said, her heart sinking. She knew she should be glad at the prospect of finally getting her Christmas break back on track, but as she peeped over her shoulder at the empty shop, her heart gave a little twang of grief.

Following him back out into the little village square, she paused to wait while he locked the gates, and then they both headed towards the pub. They were just a few feet away when the door opened wide, and warm, golden light flooded out along with the smell of fresh bacon. Caro's stomach growled in response. How could she already be hungry after such an epic breakfast?

'Sam, my love, hello!'

A beaming woman was staring at them both from the open doorway. She had a long, woollen scarf wrapped around her neck, and an army coat that she'd pulled on over a voluminous pink pinafore dress. Her wild, curly grey hair was held back with a yellow, spotty headband. She was wearing wellington boots and leaning on a large shovel. Caro liked her instantly. She looked like trouble.

'Hi Lucy, just the person. This is Caro.'

Caro stepped forward to shake the woman's spare hand but found herself wrapped in a warm, one-armed hug instead.

'Lovely to meet you Caro,' she trilled, 'what a nice surprise to see our Sam with such a gorgeous girl!'

'Oh, no...' Caro squeaked.

'It's not like that, Luce!' muttered Sam.

'Not at all!' Caro agreed.

Lucy laughed. 'All right you two, no need to look quite so horrified.'

'Can we come in and sort a couple of things out in the warm, Luce?' Sam asked quickly.

Caro shot him a look. Poor bloke! She bet he wished that he'd left her stranded in the ditch, after all the trouble she was causing him.

'Of course, my loves. You two go on in - help yourself to tea and coffee - you know your way to the kitchen Sam. I'll be in when I'm done.'

'Done with what?' he asked.

'I just need to clear the snow away from the door and the pavement at the front here before it gets trodden in too much.'

'I'll do it!' said Sam. 'You take Caro inside - she can fill you in on what's happened.'

'Oh Sam, you're an angel!' She grinned at him and relinquished her shovel at speed before he could change his mind.

'Do you want your coat back?' Caro asked.

'Nah - take it in for me. The exercise will warm me up!'

'Come on love, let's get you a drink,' said Lucy, wrapping an arm around her shoulders and marching her into the welcoming warmth of the bar.

She'd expected the place to be completely empty as it was probably only about eleven in the morning - as well as being Christmas Eve - but as her eyes accustomed to the soft lighting, she realised that there was an elderly gent sitting at the bar with a pint of stout in front of him, and another woman with two long, grey plaits was kneeling in front of the gigantic open fireplace, adding a couple of logs.

She turned to greet Lucy, and smiled as soon as she spotted Caro.

'Look who I found outside! Sue this is Caro.'

'Lovely to meet you,' said Caro, smiling as Sue got

CHRISTMAS LIGHTS AND SNOWBALL FIGHTS

to her feet and beckoned them both over to the table near the fire.

'I thought you were going to shovel the snow, Luce?' asked Sue.

'Ah, lovely Sam turned up just in the nick of time and claimed that job for himself. Cuppa, love?' she asked, turning to Caro.

'Ooh, I'd love one. Black with nothing, please.' Caro said gratefully, peeling her arms out of Sam's coat and hanging it carefully over the back of a chair.

'I'll grab you one too, Sue - before we get cracking!'

'Sounds like a plan to me,' Sue grinned.

'Can I get you another one, Alf?' she asked as she passed the gent at the bar.

'Naw lass, I'm set!' he said, raising his glass to his lips and draining the last of his pint. 'I'd better be off to help them set up for later - see you this evening!' he said getting to his feet.

'Right you are, Alf - thanks again for the sprouts!'

'Pleasure lass - I'm looking forward to it!' he said and, pulling on a thick jacket, he ambled out into the snowy square, letting in a quick blast of cold air as he went.

'Have a seat Caro!' Sue smiled warmly at her. 'What brings you here? Did I hear that right - you're staying with Sam?' she asked curiously.

Caro couldn't help but notice her tone of surprise and raised eyebrows.

'Oh, erm - no. I mean, yes - I stayed with him last night - but it wasn't planned.'

'Ooh like that, eh?!' Sue wiggled her eyebrows.

'No, no, not like that!' Caro said quickly, mortified. She could feel the blush already creeping up her neck. 'I had an accident on the lanes last night - ended up in the ditch. I was really lucky that Sam heard it and came to investigate. He helped me out of the car - but then it started snowing - so I ended up staying at his place.'

'You poor love!' said Sue. 'You're not hurt, are you?'

Caro shook her head. 'No, I'm fine. It sounds a bit more dramatic than it actually was.'

'That's good. Is your car okay?'

'I'm not actually sure. Poor old Bert is still lodged in the ditch and buried underneath a blanket of snow.'

'Who's buried under a blanket of snow?' asked Lucy, looking horrified as she plonked a tray holding three steaming mugs down onto the table.

'Caro's car!' said Sue. She quickly filled Lucy in on what she'd missed, passing Caro's mug across to her before taking her own in her hands.

'Well, imagine!' said Lucy when Sue was done.

'I was just lucky that Sam turned up otherwise I'd have been really stuffed,' said Caro, shuddering slightly at the thought. She took a sip of tea, relishing the comforting warmth of the mug in her hands.

'Bless him, he's a treasure that lad. And you say you stayed the night at his place? Well well!'

'I'm sure he'd have been much happier if I hadn't - he was pretty keen to get me out of there as quickly as possible this morning!'

'Well...' said Sue, her voice trailing away as she looked questioningly at Lucy.

'See, thing is Caro, love, Sam's had a tough time of it. Did he mention anything to you?'

Caro shook her head, looking quizzically from Sue to Lucy, willing them to carry on, but equally, not wanting to pry.

'I'm not sure it's our place to say,' said Sue in a quiet voice. 'All I *will* say is that it is very unusual for him to invite anyone into the house at all.'

'Oh, erm, right,' said Caro, now completely confused. 'Well, I'm really grateful to him. I'd have been stuck without his help.' She paused and took another sip of tea, hoping that one of them might fill the silence with a bit more information, but they both kept quiet.

'Lucy, I don't suppose it would be okay for me to use your phone, would it?' she asked after the silence had gone on for a little bit too long. 'I was on my way to my parents' place last night when it happened. I called them from Sam's to let them know - but I promised to call them again this morning to arrange a lift home.'

'You're very welcome to use the phone, but I don't think you'll be going anywhere today! Sorry my lovely, but pretty much everyone is snowed in - it's quite deep in places. They're clearing the main roads as quickly as they can, but we're due another heavy fall this evening. I'm afraid you might have to put up with us for a bit longer.'

Caro's heart sank, and it clearly showed on her face.

'Oh love, don't look so disappointed,' said Sue, patting her hand in a friendly manner. 'We're not all that bad.'

'I'm sure you're not ...' Caro smiled at her sadly.

'And we do Christmas really well!' said Lucy, putting her tea down to pat her on the shoulder.

That surprised Caro. 'I didn't think that Christmas was that big a deal here - I mean, I noticed on my way through last night that you guys don't have any lights up in the village - or a tree - or any decorations. In fact, these are the first decorations I've seen since I arrived,' she said, pointing at the swathes of greenery and red and gold baubles that were twinkling from the pub's wooden beams.

'Don't you believe it! Christmas is a huge deal here - we just have some slightly unusual traditions!' laughed Sue. 'The lights are lit for the first time on Christmas Eve. There's a whole ceremony this evening. And then they're always taken down the day after Boxing Day.'

'Wow! Why so short a time?' Caro asked, thinking of Plymouth, where Christmas had been in evidence since the end of September.

'I'm sure there's some very long, in-depth history behind it that I don't know,' said Lucy, 'and I'm sure half the parish council will be in here this evening if you really want to find out and have the pants bored off you while you're at it!'

Caro laughed. 'I'm good thanks.'

'Don't blame you!'

'I bet it's kind of nice though,' she said.

'What, getting the pants bored off you?' asked Sue with a twinkle.

'No! The fact that all the lights and celebrations are saved for just a few special days.'

Both of them nodded eagerly. 'Everyone piles in here afterwards.'

'Then, of course, most of the village have their Christmas dinner in here with me too!' said Lucy with pride.

'You're not serious?' said Caro in surprise.

'Of course! It turns into the village living-room. I've got whopping turkeys lined up and all sorts of goodies. Why do you think Sue and I are here now? We're on peeling duty! We've got to get it done early!!'

'Wow,' said Caro, her eyes shining at the idea of everyone piling in for Christmas lunch together. It was such a strange idea, but lovely too.

'Yeah - well, why should everyone bother cooking when our Luce here does it so beautifully and has the oven space to spare!'

'Sounds brilliant!' said Caro. 'Hey - I might still be here!'

'I think it's pretty much a dead cert, my love,' said

Lucy kindly, 'and there's plenty of space for you and Sam to join us!'

'Ooh I'd love to. Thank you. Erm, Lucy - I know this is asking a lot...'

'Ask away love,' Lucy grinned, downing the last of her tea.

'Well, I don't suppose you've got a room I could rent while I'm stuck here, do you?'

Lucy shook her head. 'I'm so sorry love, but with this unexpected weather, I've got all of Sue's family staying in the flat upstairs. They came for a quick visit and got stuck like you have - though not quite so dramatically!'

'And I've got the kids filling all available nooks and crannies at my cottage - I couldn't ask Luce to put up with all of them!' said Sue.

'Do either of you know anyone who might have a room available . . . or even just a sofa?'

'Sorry,' said Lucy shaking her head. 'With it being this close to Christmas, everyone has pretty much already filled up with family, or they've lent their couches out to other people who got snowed in.'

'Why don't you ask Sam if you can stay with him again?' said Sue. 'I'm sure he'd love the company.'

'I don't think so,' said Caro quickly, shaking her head. She thought about how desperate he'd been to get her out of there that morning - and the fact that he was quite so pissed-off with her right now for snooping around his workshop. 'I'll think of something,' she said, though right at that moment, she had no idea what "something" might be.

CHAPTER 7

Sam had still not reappeared by the time they'd all finished another cup of tea, so Caro decided to get on and call her parents. Maybe they'd have a different take on the whole situation. Perhaps, if the main road wasn't too bad, she could walk up to meet them somewhere along it. If not, then they needed to know that she wasn't going to make it home for Christmas as planned. She didn't want them worrying unnecessarily.

'I'm so sorry,' said her mum when she'd explained that the village was completely snowed in. 'From what we can gather, the main road is in a real state between our place and Little Bamton. They haven't had the chance to clear it yet - I think they're focusing on the dual carriageway first.' Her mum paused, listening to something her dad was mumbling in the background.

'Your dad says we're due a lot more snow this afternoon too. Best stay put.'

'Yeah - that's exactly what the girls here suggested too.'

'You'll be okay, though?' said her mum, sounding worried all of a sudden.

'Of course I will! I'm sure I'll be able to find someone to stay with.'

'I really am sorry, love.'

'Don't worry about me,' Caro smiled down the line. She could hear that her mum was worried, and disappointed that she wasn't going to make it home for the big day after all, but Caro was pretty sure that she could detect a hint of relief in there too - possibly that she wasn't going to try to brave the snowy roads.

'You sure you'll be okay there, Caro?' her mum asked again.

'Yes - everyone seems lovely. They've already invited me to the tree lighting tonight, and there's a full-on Christmas lunch at the pub tomorrow, so I'm not going to starve!' she laughed.

'Good. That's good. And you'll let us know when you've confirmed where you're staying?'

'I promise, mum,' Caro smiled. She may be a fully-grown woman, but the mum-vibe was still strong in this one.

'Good good. Oh - your dad remembered that Wills lad's first name.'

'Who?' said Caro, slightly distracted as she watched

Sam come in through the front door, pausing to stamp his feet on the doormat.

'The son of your dad's metal detecting friend who lives in Little Bamton? Maybe you'll meet him now you're going to be staying there longer! His name is Sam Wills - some kind of hot-shot designer. Makes these fancy places out of wood, apparently! Tragic story-'

'Mum, I'm really sorry, I'd better go,' Caro interrupted her mum gently. She felt a bit bad, but her spine was tingling uncomfortably. She had to be talking about her Sam. Well, not *her* Sam... but the Sam who had just reappeared and was busy laughing at something Lucy was saying. She really didn't want to hear anything that he didn't want to share with her himself - especially as she was about to beg him to have her to stay another night, if not two, in his amazing home. What other choice did she have?

'Oh, okay love, I understand. Drop me a message when you know where you're staying, and maybe give me a call tomorrow?'

She sounded uncharacteristically sad all of a sudden, and Caro felt awful. 'Of course, mum, I'll call you. Love you both - Merry Christmas!'

'You too love - try to have a good time!'

'Bye mum!'

Caro replaced the receiver and took a deep breath. Well, she'd better get this over with.

'All set?' said Sam as she headed back over to the

table where both Lucy and Sue were sitting with a monstrous pile of sprouts between them, methodically trimming them, crossing the bottoms and tossing them into a huge metal pan.

'Erm, not exactly,' she said, swallowing nervously. 'Sam, could I have a quick word a sec?' she asked, nodding to the other end of the bar. She didn't want to be rude, but she did want to give him the chance to say no in private.

'Of course, excuse us for a mo, ladies,' he said.

Lucy waved them both off and grabbed another sprout.

'What is it?' he asked in a low voice.

'Apparently everyone is pretty much snowed in. Looks like I'm going to be stuck here until tomorrow - maybe even Boxing Day.'

Sam nodded. 'Yeah - that's pretty much what Alf said to me just now too. They haven't even got to the main road along here yet - and there's more snow coming later.'

Caro nodded. A small flock of butterflies had set up camp in her stomach and she squirmed at having to ask him such a huge favour, especially now that she knew there was some kind of deep, dark secret in his past.

'Upstairs is already taken,' she said, 'and Sue said pretty much everyone she knows either has family staying or they've already taken people in.'

Sam nodded.

'Look - I know this is a massive favour to ask, especially with it being Christmas - and you've done so much already - but is there any chance I can stay with you again?'

There, she'd said it. The temptation to ramble and tell him she'd be on her best behaviour, that she'd chip in for food, and that he'd hardly know she was there was massive, but she forced herself to clamp her lips together and wait for an answer without confusing matters any further.

Sam sighed, then nodded. 'I guess you better had,' he said without a smile. 'It doesn't sound like there are any other options.'

Great. Well, at least that was that problem solved. Shame he sounded so underwhelmed by the whole idea, though.

'You've no idea how grateful I am,' she said.

Sam shook his head and forced a smile. 'It's fine. You're welcome. Look - will you be okay here for a bit? I need to go and help the guys to sort out the lights in the church yard for tonight. Alf said they were struggling a bit and could do with an extra pair of hands.'

'Oh - sure!' Caro nodded quickly.

'Great. Back in a bit.'

Sam was out of the door again before she could say another word, and Caro heaved a deep sigh before making her way back over to where Sue and Lucy were deep in conversation about mince-pie recipes.

'What have you done to the poor lad?' laughed Sue, as she slid into the chair next to her.

'Nothing!' squeaked Caro guiltily. 'Only wrecked his Christmas by gate-crashing his home!' she added.

'He agreed to you staying, then?' asked Lucy lightly.

Caro nodded. 'He seemed pretty put out by the whole thing though.'

'Ah, you'll have to give the poor lad a bit of a chance. This time of the year is especially difficult for him,' said Lucy, shaking her head with a sad expression on her face.

'What do you mean?' prompted Caro, her resolve not to stick her nose in wavering.

'Well,' said Sue, 'I guess if you're going to be staying with him for longer, it's probably better that you know - and someone else is bound to tell you if we don't.' She paused and took a deep breath. 'Sam lost his lovely wife just before Christmas a couple of years ago. They'd been together forever but hadn't been married long at all.'

Caro gasped, unable to stop herself. Poor Sam!

'This will be his third Christmas without Amy… and, well, it was her thing, you know?' said Lucy.

Sue nodded. 'She was a lovely girl - like the queen of Christmas. She got so excited - and was always right at the heart of all the celebrations here in the village.'

'That's why he finds it all so painful,' added Lucy. 'It must bring back all these memories. That first year must have been hell for him. I don't think he did anything for Christmas at all last year, and I doubt he was planning anything this year either, if I'm honest.'

The image of the un-decorated tree in Sam's sitting room flashed into Caro's mind, and she felt her heart ache for him. No, she wouldn't share that with the others - that was completely private - but somehow, it suddenly made a lot more sense. Poor, poor Sam.

'And now he's stuck with me!' she said in horror. 'Just when he needs space, and peace, and quiet.'

Sue shook her head gently. 'No Caro, what he needs is good company, friendship, and people who remind him there's still good in the world.'

Caro swallowed and nodded. She couldn't imagine what he'd been through, but she could do her best to make sure he had a Christmas to remember for happy reasons, rather than sad ones.

'Okay - thank you both - for trusting me enough to share,' she said. 'How can I repay you for being so kind?'

'Well, you can start by taking over sprout duty if you're up for it!' laughed Lucy. 'You and Sue can work your way through this lot while I get some lunch sorted out for the team that are putting up the lights ready for tonight?'

'I'll just wash my hands - then let me at 'em!' laughed Caro.

❆

When she settled back down at the table, she marvelled at the mountain of sprouts they still had to work through. But it wasn't as though she had anywhere else in the world she should - or could - be. What could be nicer than sitting by the fire with Sue and doing something to help out?

'I'm guessing these are for the village meal tomorrow?' she asked Sue as she picked up Lucy's discarded knife and set to work.

'Oh yes,' laughed Sue, 'they're not all for Lucy's tea!'

'Crikey, that must have been an epic shop at the greengrocers...'

'Oh no - these are from the village allotment. Old Alf who was in here just now, he grows them for the meal every year. It's become a bit of a tradition. Actually, a lot of the veg for tomorrow comes from the allotments.'

'Wow - I love that!' said Caro in awe. 'It's a really tight-knit community here then?'

'Oh, you'd better believe it!' grinned Sue. 'You'll be able to meet them all at lunch tomorrow - that's if you haven't already met everyone by the end of today anyway!' she laughed.

'I'm really looking forward to it. I couldn't expect Sam to feed me!'

'Like Lucy said, there's plenty of room for both of you tomorrow.'

'That's brilliant,' said Caro. 'Though Sam might have other plans, of course!'

'Between the two of us, I'm pretty sure his plans

probably involve a frozen pizza and a couple of beers in front of the TV,' she said sadly.

'Well - let's change that!' said Caro.

'Hey, did he show you his workshop while you were at his place? It's amazing in there.'

'I got a quick glimpse of the one at the house,' said Caro, grabbing yet another sprout, 'and he showed me around the craft centre just now.'

She decided not to tell Sue about her faux pas with the angel carving earlier. She still wasn't one hundred percent sure what that had been about, but after everything she'd heard about Sam since entering the pub, she guessed that it would have something to do with losing Amy.

'Oh, I love the craft centre,' said Sue. 'Isn't Sam's furniture gorgeous?'

Caro nodded enthusiastically. 'I fell in love with this little table. I don't usually get that excited about furniture - I'm more of an Ikea girl - but those pieces are incredible!'

Sue nodded in agreement. 'He certainly has a way with wood, that boy!'

'I'm surprised they don't open on Christmas Eve, though,' said Caro.

'They would, normally - but there's not much point when no one can get here I guess!' said Sue, chuckling.

Caro rolled her eyes at her own stupidity. 'Duh! Of course. So, who owns it all - I mean, who's the landlord?'

'The vicar manages it, believe it or not,' said Sue. 'The buildings belong to the church, and all the rent goes towards the upkeep of the church, village grounds, that kind of thing.'

Caro didn't understand why, but her heart was hammering. The vicar? If it was a charitable kind of set up, maybe the rent wouldn't be too high?

'You okay, Caro?' asked Sue, one eyebrow raised.

'Oh, yeah. Of course. I was just thinking about that little empty unit...'

'Ooh, you interested? It would be so good to get that filled.'

Caro nodded. Yes, she was more than interested.

'Well, let's get these sprouts finished up, and I'll take you over to meet Mark, our vicar. He's a lovely bloke - I expect he's over there helping to set up the lights.'

Caro swallowed. Now, really? Wasn't that all a bit sudden? Didn't that make it all a bit real?

'Don't look so scared,' said Sue kindly. 'No harm in asking, right?'

'You're right. Thanks Sue!'

CHAPTER 8

It took the two of them a surprisingly short amount of time to get to the bottom of the sprout mountain. While Sue pulled on her coat, Caro nipped out into the pub kitchen to find Lucy, deliver the sprouts and let her know where they were headed.

'We'll be back in a bit,' she said.

'Okay love. Thanks for your help with these. Could you let the gang know that there's bacon sarnies, mince pies and hot drinks here for them whenever they're ready.'

'Yum! Okay, will do.'

'You too, Caro - you're one of the team now,' she grinned.

Caro felt a lump form in her throat. She swallowed hard, hoping to mask the strange swell of emotion, but she wasn't quick enough to hide it from Lucy.

'Oh love! You okay?' she asked. She looked like she

wanted to reach forward and hug her, but Caro was incredibly grateful that she didn't - she wasn't sure she'd have held it together otherwise.

'I'm good,' she laughed. 'Sorry, not sure what that was about!'

'It's Christmas, and not the one you were expecting,' said Lucy wisely.

'Yeah. But I got to meet you guys, so it's all good,' Caro smiled.

As she headed back out into the bar, Sue was waiting for her by the door. As an afterthought, Caro quickly snagged Sam's coat from the back of the chair. He must be cold by now!

As they crossed the snowy square towards the stone church, Sue pointed out the little lane that ran between the vicarage and the side of the craft centre.

'That's the village allotments up there,' she said.

'Wow, not many food miles in tomorrow's veg, then!' said Caro.

'Nope - just a few food feet. And though we call them allotments, it's more of a community garden really. We were all so busy sharing the crops between us anyway, we decided that it was better just to share the space, grow things communally - and it's worked really well.'

'I'm guessing you're involved?' Caro asked.

'Oh yes - that place is like my baby. I spend so much time in there!'

Suddenly, Caro came to an abrupt halt. She'd just

spotted the tree that had been erected in front of the church.

'Okay, wow! Now that's a tree!'

Sue chuckled. 'She's a beauty, isn't she?!'

'Don't tell me you grew that on the allotments too?'

'Hardly!' Sue snorted. 'Didn't Sam tell you - he's sponsored the tree for years, or, I should say, his company has.'

As if Sue had summoned him by mentioning his name, Sam came into view as he uncoiled a huge rope of lights for another man, who was tucking them into the lower branches of the tree, one metre at a time.

As if sensing their eyes on him, Sam looked over his shoulder and spotted them.

'Hi! Everything okay?'

'All good, thanks Sam!' said Sue.

'Okay. Good. Sorry I abandoned you for a bit Caro - we're nearly done though.'

'I don't mind - I've been having my own fun preparing a sprout-mountain for our lunch tomorrow!' she said.

'*Our* lunch? I'm afraid I've not booked . . .' Sam said, going back to uncoiling his lights with more attention than was strictly necessary.

'I'll just go find the vicar,' Sue muttered, and quickly walked off towards the open front door of the church. Caro got the distinct impression that she was trying to give them a bit of privacy. Weird.

'Well, I wasn't sure what your plans were, and I

didn't want to be even more of a burden to you than I am already, so when Lucy said I could go - I accepted. I hope you don't mind?' she said,

'Oh . . . well, of course I don't!' he said as he finally handed the end of the lead over to the other guy and wandered over to stand with her. 'Good tree this year,' he said distractedly.

'It really is - so generous of you,' she said.

'Oh. Erm, well . . . just doing my bit, you know.'

Caro peeped sideways at him. He looked uncomfortable again.

'Lucy said there's plenty of room for both of us for lunch tomorrow, by the way. Only if you fancy it, of course?'

Sam cleared his throat, still staring at the tree. 'Well, Lucy is probably the best cook I know, so it would be pretty stupid to turn down an offer like that.' He rubbed his arms and stamped his feet, clearly feeling the cold now that he'd stopped working.

'Here,' said Caro, remembering that she had his coat folded over one arm.

'Ah, great - thanks!' he said gratefully, pulling it straight on.

'Speaking of Lucy - she wanted me to tell you that there's bacon sarnies, mince pies and a hot drink waiting for you all when you're ready.'

'Now that is music to my ears,' grinned Sam. 'I'm starving.'

'I can't believe I'm saying this after that incredible breakfast you made me, but me too!' agreed Caro.

'Look, we've got a couple of things left to do here, and then we'll be over. Why don't you head back to the pub - at least you'll be warm!' said Sam.

'I will in just a sec, but I think Sue wanted to introduce me to the vicar - and I'd love to take a quick peek inside the church while I'm here.'

'Go for it. See you back at the pub in a bit. Though, I'm warning you, it's colder inside that Church than it is out here!'

Caro left Sam to hunting through a massive, plastic trug full of industrial-looking cables, and headed for the door of the church. Sam was right - as she stepped through the doors, she could have sworn that the temperature dropped by a degree or two.

The little church was beautiful inside. The bright, white morning light that was being reflected by the snow outside showed off the colours in the magnificent stained glass. Caro came to a halt, staring at the largest window behind the pulpit.

'Breathtaking, isn't it,' said a man's low voice right next to her.

Caro turned quickly to find a pair of very blue eyes twinkling at her. She nodded and smiled, not wanting to be rude. If this was the vicar, he wasn't exactly what she'd been expecting. He was wearing a flat-cap for one thing, and a waxed, Barbour jacket. And wellington boots! But then she spotted the dog-collar peeking out from under the unusual outer layer, and her suspicions were confirmed.

'You must be Caro?' he asked, holding out his hand politely.

Caro nodded again and took his large, warm hand and shook it.

'You'll have to forgive my informal dress - I'm not strictly on duty this morning - though a vicar is never really off duty,' he stopped and chuckled at his own joke. 'But I know how very wet and cold these things can get, so I layered up.'

'Good call!' said Caro, finally finding her voice. 'It's gorgeous out there, but pretty chilly! Sam's already had to come to my rescue by lending me his coat earlier.'

'He's a good man, our Sam,' the vicar smiled.

Caro couldn't help but notice that every single person who'd mentioned Sam so far had nothing but love for him. He was clearly an adored member of the community here.

'So I'm told. And he saved me from a very cold night stuck in a ditch, so I definitely owe him one.'

'Ah, yes. Sue told me - I'm sorry to hear about your accident. I'm so glad that you weren't hurt.'

'I'm fine,' Caro said. 'Just sad that I won't be able to celebrate Christmas with my parents this year.'

The vicar nodded solemnly. 'Yes - family is important, especially at this time of the year. But don't forget - no matter what you believe in - Christmas has a certain magic to it. You might find that you were meant to spend your Christmas here with us in Little Bamton.'

Caro smiled at his kind words. She knew he was only trying to make her feel better about being stuck here, but something in what he said lodged somewhere deeper inside her than she'd have expected.

'And on that note,' he said, his voice sounding a little less grave, 'Sue tells me that you're interested in finding out more about the craft centre?'

'Oh, well . . . yes! I mean, I don't know if I'd be able to actually . . . you know. . . act on anything,' Caro paused and swallowed. Why the hell was she suddenly feeling so nervous?

'It doesn't do any harm to find out the details though, does it?' he smiled at her kindly. 'Then you can have a think about it and see if the empty unit is something that might work for you.'

Caro nodded enthusiastically. 'That's what Sue said too.'

'So what sort of thing do you do, Caro?' he asked, indicating for her to take a seat in the pew nearest to where they were still standing.

She sat down and slid along to make room for him too. He took off his cap and brushed his salt and pepper hair back off his forehead, giving her his undivided attention. It was actually quite nerve-wracking!

'I work in a shop at the moment,' she started, 'but it's always been my dream to own my own vintage shop. But that's not all I'd sell - I make my own accessories. I love up-cycling, and creating my own designs out of vintage fabrics too.'

'Well, that does sound like something that would be an incredible addition to the businesses that are already tenants - and I think that's important. I do my best to make sure that there aren't too many cross-overs - it's best that we have a wide range of crafts there.'

'Yes, I noticed when Sam showed me around earlier that there's a brilliant mix of different things for sale.'

'So much talent!' said the vicar proudly. 'Well, if you'd like, I can take your email address and I'll send you over all the details about the empty unit. It won't be until after Christmas now, I'm afraid - things get a bit hectic for me around this time of year!'

'I bet,' laughed Caro. 'I'd love that. And thank you so much for taking the time to chat.'

'Always a pleasure. If you like the look of the terms after you've had a chance to read through the pack, we can always arrange a time for you to have another visit - a day when everyone's open so that you can meet them all and have a proper look inside the space.'

Caro's heart leapt. That sounded amazing.

'Now then,' he said, getting to his feet and settling his flat cap back in place, 'did I hear mention of bacon sandwiches and mince pies?'

CHAPTER 9

It had been the weirdest Christmas Eve afternoon Caro had ever had. There hadn't been a single last-minute gift for her to wrap - by now she was usually ensconced in a quiet corner somewhere, battling with the cello-tape and trying not to get it caught in her hair for the thousandth time as she wrestled with sparkly paper and wayward bows.

Instead, there had been bacon sandwiches with the tree-light crew, followed by the most mouth-watering mince pies she'd ever tasted. Caro was definitely going to miss Lucy's baking when she returned to real life.

Lucy sidled up to her as she tucked into her third one.

'You know, this is the longest I've seen Sam hang out with everyone since Amy died,' she whispered in her ear, 'and I think it's the happiest I've seen him too. You're definitely doing that boy some kind of good.'

'I've barely seen him,' Caro tried to laugh Lucy's comment off as she swallowed her mouthful of crumbly pastry and mincemeat, but she couldn't help the blush from spreading across her cheeks. 'I don't think I can take any credit!'

'You mark my words, you crash-landing into his Christmas might be just the thing that boy needed.' She winked at Caro and ambled off back towards the kitchen, no doubt to brew another pot of tea and pull out yet more of her delicious pies.

'Hey Caro!' said Sam, catching her eye and edging his way through the crush over towards her. 'You doing okay?' Maybe he'd sensed they'd been talking about him.

'Great, thanks,' she smiled, feeling slightly guilty. Maybe Lucy had a point - he *did* look more relaxed than she'd seen him so far. Perhaps being in the unexpected company of half the village was giving him a break from all the difficult memories.

'That's good,' he nodded. 'Look - there are a few things I need to go and do.'

'Oh - right . . .'

'Sorry-'

'Don't apologise Sam!' she smiled at him again. 'I've completely gatecrashed your Christmas - of course there are things you have planned.'

He shifted his weight awkwardly and stared at his feet for a minute. 'So, ah, you'll be okay down here for a bit?'

She nodded. Her stomach lurched with unexpected nerves at the thought of him not being around somewhere nearby, but it wasn't as though he could babysit her all afternoon.

'Of course. I'm looking forward to watching the tree lighting later. I'm sure there's something I can do in here to help Lucy in the meantime. I'll find my way back to your place afterwards.'

Sam shook his head. 'Actually, I think I'll pop down for the lighting myself. I've missed it for the last couple of years.'

He paused, looking confused and awkward for a moment, and Caro wondered if he was going to tell her about Amy. But there was a sudden loud cheer at the other end of the bar, followed by a wave of laughter, and it seemed to change his mind.

'So . . . ah yeah, I thought I'd come this evening,' he said again.

'Okay.'

'Yeah. So, I'll meet you in here beforehand? And then we'll either brave the Land Rover and try getting back up the hill, or figure something else out.'

'Sounds like a plan. See you later.'

'Have fun, Caro.' Sam quickly buttoned up his coat, and without another word to anyone, headed straight for the door.

'Where's he off to?' asked Sue, appearing at Caro's shoulder.

Caro shrugged. 'Said he had a few things to do this afternoon.'

'So he's just abandoned you?'

'I'd hardly call this abandonment,' laughed Caro, raising her half-eaten mince pie in a salute.

'Don't worry - we'll make sure we get you home safely later.'

'No need. He's coming back in time for the lighting ceremony.'

'You're kidding!' gasped Sue. 'Well, Lucy was right, you're having a good effect on that boy!'

'Hardly,' said Caro. 'Anyway, he's just landed you and Luce with babysitting duties for the afternoon.'

'Well, why don't you come and meet some more people? See that woman who's just come in? That's Amber who makes the amazing willow sculptures! Oh, and that's Lyndon coming in behind her. You definitely need to meet him,' said Sue, excitedly pulling at Caro's arm.

Several hours later, Caro's face was flushed from the warmth of the pub's open fire and the crush of the villagers who'd been arriving steadily all afternoon.

She'd recounted her story about ending up in the ditch and Sam coming to her rescue more times than she could count, and the tale had already started to take on a life of its own. She'd overheard one little girl telling her brother that Sam was a superhero and had rushed that "new girl" to hospital. No doubt by tomorrow morning, the story would have reached epic-movie-proportions.

Craving a moment to herself and a bit of peace and quiet, she ducked out of the little knot of people standing around her with a quick smile and decided to clear some empties as an excuse to escape to the kitchen.

'Thanks lovely, but you don't need to do that - you're my guest!' Lucy greeted her with a grin as she carefully loaded the tray of glasses into one of the massive dishwashers.

'It's no problem - seriously, I'm glad to help. You're heaving out there. And, if I'm honest, I need a quick break. Everyone's lovely, but I seem to have inadvertently managed to become some kind of celebrity.'

Lucy laughed. 'You're new and exciting - nothing really happens here, so you're huge news! Don't mind them, they're just being friendly in their own weird ways.'

Caro laughed. 'I really don't mind - just needed a couple of minutes somewhere quiet. It's been a weird couple of days.'

'Well you don't have to buy your way back here with empties!' laughed Lucy.

'Good to know,' Caro grinned back at her, 'but as I'm here, is there anything I can do to help you out for a bit?'

'You're like a Christmas angel.'

'I'll take that! I've been called a lot worse.'

'Well, if you're serious, there's the rest of the veg to prepare for tomorrow. How do you feel about carrot duty?'

❄

How? How was it nearly five in the evening already? Caro popped her knife down and swept the last stack of chopped carrots into a huge silver pan. She pushed her fringe out of her eyes with the back of her hand and stretched her back.

She was so grateful to Lucy for giving her a sanctuary back here, but with the carrots done she guessed she'd better show her face and be sociable again. It was nearly time for the tree lighting anyway.

Maybe Sam would be back by now. She smiled softly to herself at the thought, then gave herself a stern shake. Totally. Inappropriate. Thoughts. Especially after what she'd learned about him today. But she couldn't deny that he intrigued her - there was clearly a very kind man under the layers of protective grumpiness. An image of a chunky slice of fruit cake with a birthday candle sticking out of the top crossed her mind's eye and she grinned.

'Get a grip, Caro,' she muttered to herself, quickly stripping off the comedy elf apron Lucy had loaned her and smoothing down her hair.

She stepped back out into the bar, expecting to find the same heaving crowd she'd escaped an hour ago.

Much to her surprise, there was only a handful of people left, finishing off pints or pulling on scarves and jackets.

She spotted Sue, who was still over near her table by the fireplace, chatting away to the vicar.

'Where on earth did you disappear to?' she asked as Caro reached them. 'Thought we'd scared you off!'

Caro grinned sheepishly. 'I ran away to the kitchen and carrot duty!'

'You didn't have to do all that - you're meant to be having a good time! You're our guest!'

'I am having a good time. A great time, actually,' smiled Caro.

'Just needed a quiet few minutes to process, eh?' the vicar smiled at her kindly and she grinned back.

'You could say that!'

'I can imagine. Little Bamton is nothing if not friendly, but it can be a lot to take if you're not used to it!' he laughed. 'I remember when I first arrived, I used to disappear into the vestry and lock the door for half an hour - just to get a moment to myself.'

'Aha!' said Sue, 'your secret's out. I always said that a collection of bibles didn't need dusting that often!'

'And on that note,' the vicar laughed, 'shall we head over to the church? It must be nearly time for the lights!'

'You ready, Caro?' asked Sue, pulling a massive green bobble hat down over her grey plaits and stuffing her arms into a red duffle coat.

'Have you seen Sam? He said he'd meet me in here…' she said.

'Ah, don't worry about that. He's probably been held up or got roped in to helping with something on his way over,' said Sue, and the vicar nodded.

'Come over with us - I'm sure you'll catch up with him over there,' she said kindly, though Caro didn't miss the quick look between the two of them. It was obvious that they didn't really believe Sam would turn up, even though he said he was going to be there.

Just as she was about to say that she'd rather wait here, Lucy started ushering all the other stragglers out of the pub.

'Okay you lot, you know the drill - I'm closing up for the ceremony. Feel free to leave your stuff here if you want to - I'll turn the key in the door behind us, and I'll open up as soon as we're done!'

Caro quickly grabbed her jacket, wishing she had the comfort of Sam's thick coat instead.

'Caro, love?' said Lucy bustling over to her, 'would you like to borrow this?' She held out a cherry-red padded jacket. 'It gets pretty cold, standing around out there!'

'Ohhh, thank you!' she said gratefully, pulling it on and snuggling into it.

They were just bundling out of the door when Sam appeared.

'I'm so sorry I'm late - I got caught up with… something,' he said, tailing off abruptly.

Caro grinned up at him. 'That's okay - we're just on our way over. Everything okay?'

Sam nodded, and she fell into step beside him. The snow in the square had already been compacted down by everyone traipsing over it from the pub to the church yard, and Caro slipped more than once as they made their way across towards the church yard gates.

She did her best not to squeal every time it happened, but she was getting slower and slower.

'Here,' said Sam, and with a sigh, he offered her his arm. Caro took it gratefully, instantly feeling a bit more secure knowing that he'd stop her from landing on her bum.

She was about to thank him when she caught Lucy's eye as she overtook them, walking with Sue and the vicar. Lucy wiggled her eyebrows and gave Caro a wink, and she felt the heat rise to her cheeks. She would have let go of Sam's arm if she dared to, but frankly, she'd take a little light teasing over a bruised bottom any day!

When they reached the church gates, Sam paused at the table that had been set up just inside.

'Hello Molly!' he said to a little girl, who was grinning up at him, two golden plaits poking out from beneath her multi-coloured bobble hat.

'Hi Sam!' she lisped. 'Do you and your *girlfriend* want a candle?'

'I . . . uh . . .' Sam stuttered, promptly dropping Caro's arm.

'Sorry Sam!' the woman standing next to Molly, presumably her mother, cut in. 'She's obsessed with girlfriends and boyfriends at the moment. I mean, she's *six!* Her dad's already having kittens about when she becomes a teenager.'

Caro chuckled. 'We'd love a candle please Molly,' she said quickly to cover Sam's obvious discomfort.

Molly beamed at her and handed over two tapers with little cardboard collars around their stems for catching the wax.

'Thanks... do we light them here? Sorry, it's my first time.'

'No silly,' said Molly. 'Later.'

'Okay - thanks Molly,' laughed Sam,

'They're so cute at that age!' said Caro as they wound their way along the path towards the snowy front lawn where the tree stood.

'Oh yeah - curious about everything!' agreed Sam, sounding slightly bemused. 'Do you have any?' he asked.

'Me? No!' she squeaked, looking horrified. But then she realised that they hadn't discussed anything personal at all. How was he supposed to know? 'I mean - I've not really given it that much thought. I guess I've just never been with anyone who who's made me consider kids... I'm not saying I *wouldn't...*'

Stop. Talking. Caro. She cringed. What if he'd wanted kids with Amy? What if they had kids and she just didn't know...?

'Erm, do you have kids?' she asked awkwardly, as they came into sight of the crowd gathered around the dark hulk of the enormous Christmas tree.

'No,' Sam said quietly. 'No kids.'

Caro could hear the sadness in his voice and wished she hadn't asked. But then that would have been even weirder considering that he didn't know that Sue and Lucy had filled her in about losing Amy.

Just as she was hastily trying to think of a less controversial, heartbreaking subject, a single voice rose in song, and the gathered crowd in front of them fell silent.

'Come on,' whispered Sam, taking her arm again and gently leading her forward to join the rest of the village.

CHAPTER 10

Caro felt goosebumps rise on her arms that had nothing to do with the snow lying all around them. She watched as a young lad, completely dressed in white, emerged from the doors of the church. He held a single, flickering candle in his hands, and his high, clear voice brought tears to her eyes. Silent Night had never had this effect on her before.

As he slowly made his way down the path towards them, the crowd didn't make a sound. It was as though they had been spellbound by the beauty of the young voice.

When he came to the end of the first verse, he paused on the path, and a small tribe of kids appeared from the church, each of them bearing flickering lights in their hands, joining in with the soloist.

Caro grinned when she spotted Molly amongst them. The little girl waved at her and Sam excitedly as she passed them, and Caro winced as the candle she was holding tilted precariously and wobbled all over the place - coming scarily close to the bobble hat of the girl in front of her.

'LEDs,' Sam breathed in her ear, obviously catching the slight look of panic on her face. 'Lesson learned the hard way!'

Caro grinned at him and breathed a little sigh of relief. Yes - she could see now that, other than the first, slightly older boy, all the other kids were clutching fake candles.

They watched as the little procession made an inner circle around the base of the Christmas tree, turning to look out at the crowd as they finished their song.

A tall, dark figure stepped forward, looking slightly sinister in the dim, flickering light of the children's candles. Caro just about recognised the build of the vicar before he started speaking in his gentle voice.

'Every year we come here, and every year the message is the same. Let the light of Christmas kindle inside you. Let it catch in your hearts and warm your own homes first. That way, it will shine out and bless all those around you, making our village, our country, and the rest of the world a more special place.'

Caro shifted her weight in the dark. She wasn't sure what she'd been expecting, but it definitely hadn't been this. She'd assumed that there would be a countdown and lots of cheering as the Christmas tree lights flickered to life.

Instead, she was watching in awed silence as the vicar held out his candle, and the one lad with the bare flame lit it for him. Then they both turned to light another candle, and gradually the faces of the villagers came to life as the light of that single flame spread between all the candles in the church yard.

'Caro?' said Sam gently. She turned to find him standing with his own newly lit candle held out in front of him for her to light her own.

She stepped forward and tilted her wick. He cupped a hand around the wavering flames as Caro's candle caught from his own. She glanced up at him, watching his serious face as he focused on shielding the flames in front of him, and suddenly found that she couldn't look away.

He caught her eye and smiled briefly before straightening up and dropping his hand.

'There you go,' he said simply.

She smiled, swallowing hard. Her heart was doing something strange. She wasn't sure if it was the magic of this little ceremony, surrounded by all these friendly people doing what they did every Christmas, or if it was the sad, soft smile that she'd seen playing on Sam's lips - but she was feeling something she was pretty sure she shouldn't be.

'Now!' cried the vicar, mercifully demanding that she return her attention back to the front. 'Who thinks it's time to light the tree?'

A cheer went up from all the kids, and it seemed that the more sombre part of the proceedings was over.

'I can't hear you!' he shouted, and the kids all cried out again, this time joined by a good number of adults in the crowd too - including Sam, much to her amusement.

'Three!' shouted the vicar, clearly relishing his new role as pantomime-style ringmaster.

'Two!' replied the crowd.

'One!' they all cheered together.

For one beautifully blinding moment, they all stared in awe as the tree was illuminated by lights of every colour. A cheer went up.

And then it all went dark. The lights went out and the cheer turned into a massive groan of disappointment.

'Be right back!' Sam muttered in her ear, making her jump. She quickly took his candle from him and turned to watch as he jogged off towards the church. What on earth?

There was quite a lot of muttered confusion around her as everyone tried to figure out what on earth was going on. Then, from the direction of the church, she heard Sam's voice yell - 'THREE!'

A few people in the crowd, slightly confused by now replied, 'two?'

'One!' yelled Sam's disembodied voice.

As if by magic, the tree lights sprang to life again. The cheer from the crowd was twice as loud as the first time around, and it was followed by a warm round of laughter and applause.

As if everyone knew exactly what was due to happen next, voices around her started singing "Oh, Christmas Tree."

Caro gazed around her in delight, only half joining in as she took in the happy, pink faces. She saw Lucy and Sue, standing just a few feet away, clutching their candles and singing their hearts out as they gazed at the tree.

Sam reappeared, coming to stand beside her again, a little out of breath after his dash through the dark. She grinned at him and gave him a thumbs up as she handed his candle back. He gave her a little wink and added his deep voice to the rest of them.

❄

Caro couldn't stop grinning as she stared at the sloping sides of her bedroom ceiling back at Sam's cabin. She was glad to be in her cosy, borrowed pyjamas and snuggled down under the duvet - though she couldn't get over the fact that she was here - in a stranger's home - on Christmas Eve night.

It really had been the most unexpected, wonderfully weird day. After the tree had been lit, and then lit again, there had been a lot more singing and laughter in the church yard before they'd all traipsed back into the square.

Sam had laughed at the delight on Caro's face when she realised that it wasn't just the tree that had been switched on, but that the entire square was now wreathed in beautiful white lights that extended throughout the entire lower village.

Lucy had outdone herself and, opening up the pub, she ladled out gallons of the most delicious mulled wine Caro had ever tasted. She'd taken her first one gingerly from Sam and had sipped it out of politeness - expecting the usual hit of vinegar combined with a bit of cinnamon trying to mask the cheapest of cheap red wine - but how wrong had she been?! This had been warm, fruity, spicy and delicious. And, as it turned out, surprisingly alcoholic!

It really had been the perfect evening, chatting to the villagers in the snowy, newly lit square, snuggled into her borrowed jacket.

The second snowstorm they'd been expecting hadn't arrived, and though Sam had been fairly sure that the Land Rover would have gotten them both home safely, he decided that, after the mulled wine, the same thing couldn't be said for him. Sue had happily stepped into the breach having stuck to her favourite hot chocolate all night, and dropped them both home in her truck. Well, home for Sam. Back to a stranger's house for her.

Actually, maybe not such a stranger after all. Caro already felt like she'd known Sam for ages - did they really only meet yesterday?

As soon as they'd been left alone, the comfortable, relaxed vibe between them had disappeared into thin air, and they'd both gone to their separate rooms having barely shared more than a dozen words.

Caro didn't mind though. She had a feeling that this evening had taken more out of him than she would ever understand. There had been a few times she'd looked over and caught a sad, wistful expression on his face, and could only guess that he was re-living happier Christmases gone by.

Now, as she lay in his spare room, her heart ached for what he must have gone through. What must it be like to lose the other half of you?

She sighed and the room swayed gently around her. Blimey that mulled wine had had a kick to it! She only hoped that she didn't end up with the hangover from hell for Christmas day.

Christmas day. Christmas. Shit. She didn't have anything to give Sam for Christmas, and there was literally nothing she could do about it. The only things she had with her were still buried under a blanket of snow in the back of Bert - and she didn't think he'd appreciate the Old Spice gift set she'd picked up for her dad anyway!

Caro wracked her brains. There must be something she could do. He'd been so kind to her, letting her stay even though this was clearly such a tough time for him.

Caro sat bolt upright. There *was* something she could do to show how much she appreciated everything he'd done for her. He'd seemed so at home amongst the village celebrations and she'd seen enough to know that he *did* love this time of year, even though it was tinged with so much sadness.

She quietly flicked on the little bedside lamp and hopped out of bed. Pausing briefly to pull on the thick pair of welly socks Sam had lent her earlier, she climbed carefully and quietly down the spiral staircase into the sitting room.

It must be just after midnight. Sam had banked up the wood-burner before they'd gone to bed to make sure that they'd wake up to a warm house. Now, the large space was lit by the flickering glow that shone through its glass doors.

Caro padded over to the corner and flicked the switch on a standard lamp - she needed a bit more light to work by, but didn't want to run the risk of turning on the bright ceiling lights and waking Sam.

She went to stand in front of the large, bare Christmas tree, her eyes darting from it, down to the box of ornaments and back again. Now that she was down here, she wasn't as sure of her plan as she had been under the warmth of her duvet, with the buzz of Lucy's fortified mulled wine coursing through her veins. Maybe she should just forget the whole thing and go back to bed. Christmas was clearly a tough topic for Sam… would he take this the wrong way?

Caro knelt down on the floor in front of the tree

and, still completely undecided, pulled the box towards her.

She moved a strand of tinsel to one side and, reaching in, lifted a delicate glass icicle from its protective tray. She held it up, letting the lamplight glisten from its surfaces. Tentatively, as if in some kind of trance, Caro reached out and gently hung it from one of the green boughs. It was perfect.

Looking back to the box, she carefully lifted the rest of that tray out onto the floor to peep at what was underneath. She felt like a child discovering some kind of magical sweet shop. Caro had always loved decorating the Christmas tree when she was a kid, and would spend hours with her mum, talking about the history of each of the baubles as they painstakingly chose a special spot for each one.

She swallowed a lump in her throat as she wondered whether Sam had done the same with Amy. Some of these ornaments were clearly vintage, and Caro wondered if the couple had collected them or whether they'd been handed down from various family members.

She sighed. Sam had clearly intended to decorate the tree... maybe it had just been too much for him to face... one memory too many to deal with. She took in another deep breath. She would do it. It would be her small gift to him. And she hadn't had the chance to decorate a tree for so many years.

Choosing a box of delicate, vintage baubles in rich,

glossy colours, she gently hung them spaced out across the whole tree, admiring the way they seemed to catch the low lamp light, sending it dancing back across the room in a thousand tiny golden beams.

Next, she took the glass icicles and dotted them around. Wait! She couldn't go any further without getting the lights on there. She should have done that first! She started to gently set the rest of the box's contents aside as she hunted through for a string of lights. She prayed that Sam owned a modern set, even if everything else in there was an antique.

She'd almost reached the tangle of wires at the bottom when she spotted a bauble that was clearly hand-painted, with looping red and gold handwriting wrapped around the gleaming green of the background.

She lifted it out and held it up to the light to examine it closer.

For my Sam on our first Christmas.
Let's grow old together. Axxx

Something over by the doorway caught her eye, and she lowered the bauble slowly only to meet Sam's incredulous stare.

'What the hell are you doing?' he said, his voice flat and quiet.

CHAPTER 11

'I . . . I . . .' Caro stuttered, her throat closing in panic. She couldn't take her eyes off Sam. She couldn't work out whether he was angry or just surprised to find a relative stranger snooping around in his sitting room in the wee small hours of Christmas morning.

Sam strode towards her, and she braced herself for his anger. Instead he just stopped in front of her and, reaching down, he gently took the bauble and turned it over in his hands.

Caro watched as a wave of emotion crossed his face. She saw the clench and release of his jaw and the deep swallow as he wrestled with his feelings.

'Sam, I'm so sorry. I didn't mean to upset you . . . I just wanted to do something nice for you for Christmas. I didn't have anything to give you as a present, and I saw that you hadn't had the . . . erm . . . the chance to do your tree. And so . . . so I thought . . . I thought I could do it for you. As a surprise . . .' she trailed off, and finally looked away from him. She felt awful. What had she been thinking?

'Amy always did the tree,' he said quietly.

She looked back at him. He still hadn't taken his eyes off the bauble in his hands and was turning it so that the writing caught the light. Caro didn't say anything. Sam hadn't told her that he'd been married, let alone that he'd lost his wife. She didn't know what to say.

'She loved Christmas,' he continued, looking up at the partially decorated tree. 'She was like a little kid with it - and she always swept me along with her.'

He glanced at Caro, and she could see so much pain on his face that she wanted to hug him.

'Amy was my wife,' he said.

Caro nodded. 'I know,' she said gently. There was no point pretending that she didn't.

'Of course,' he said, his lip quirking at the corner for the briefest of moments, 'the joys of small-village life.'

'Lucy and Sue only told me the basics. I don't think they wanted me to put my foot in it by mistake.'

Sam nodded and sighed. He didn't seem angry, just incredibly tired.

'Sam, I really am sorry - for what happened, I mean - but for this too,' she gestured at the half-done tree. 'I can put everything back. It won't take a moment.'

Sam looked back down at the bauble again. 'No,' he said gently. 'Let's finish it - together.'

Caro looked at him in surprise and watched as a sad smile spread across his face.

'For Amy. I think she'd have liked that.'

'For Amy,' Caro said. Bending down to lift the jumble of lights out of the box, she turned and held them out to him. 'First things first... any idea where to start with these?'

'If we're going to do this in true Amy style, that is definitely *not* the place to start,' said Sam, gently placing the handwritten ornament down on the coffee table and visibly pulling himself together.

'Tinsel first?' Caro asked, confused.

'Nope. She always said that the only way to start dressing a tree was with a hot chocolate piled high with marshmallows and squirty cream,' he grinned and shook his head at what was clearly a very dear memory. 'Can I tempt you?'

'Who am I to argue with the Queen of Christmas?' Caro replied gently. 'That's what Lucy called Amy, you know?'

'She got that just about right,' said Sam. 'Come on, let's do her proud.'

❄

They both stood back to admire their handy work.

'What do you think? Would Amy like it?' asked Caro.

Whereas just an hour ago this question would have been incredibly difficult to ask, Caro now felt like she was asking about a friend. While they'd worked, Sam had started to tell her little stories about their life together. Each ornament had seemed to trigger another happy memory, and as Caro had asked him questions, he'd opened up more than ever, painting a picture of a happy life full of love and laughter.

She'd deliberately not asked him how Amy had died. Sam seemed so happy to be reliving all the precious memories of their life together, and she didn't want to spoil that.

'You know what, I think she would have loved it,' he said at last, nodding at the tree.

Caro turned to smile at him and then spotted the handwritten ornament still sitting on the coffee table.

'We've missed one,' she said, pointing to it.

Sam went over and picked it up.

'She made this for me the first Christmas we were together,' he said, the brittle crack in his voice causing Caro's heart to squeeze in sympathy. 'She asked me to marry her as she hung it on the tree. I thought she was joking and we just laughed about it - she was always laughing. But then, every single year when she hung this bauble, she'd ask me the same question. Until finally, five years later, I said yes.' Sam swallowed hard, and two fat tears rolled down his cheeks. He hurriedly wiped them away with the arm of his sweater.

Caro wanted to reach out to him, to comfort him, but this pain was too personal for her to intrude. So she stayed quiet, waiting for him to carry on speaking as she stared at the lights glinting from the tree.

'We were married in the spring. And then there was the cancer. We didn't get another Christmas together,' he said, his voice tight with barely suppressed emotion.

'Oh Sam,' Caro breathed, and reached out to gently place a hand on his arm.

'It's okay,' he said, his voice quivering. 'I'm okay.' He stepped forward and carefully hung the ornament right at the front of the tree, twisting it to make sure the words were visible before bowing his head for a moment, then stepping back.

'Sorry about that,' he said, clearing his throat.

'Don't apologise,' Caro murmured. 'I'm the one who should be saying sorry. I meant this to be a nice surprise for you - a present. I really didn't mean to upset you.'

Sam turned to look at her. 'I've not talked about Amy for a long time. This has helped me remember all the amazing moments we had together instead of the dark stuff at the end - the stuff that takes over.' He paused to look at the tree once more. 'This is the most precious gift anyone could have given me.'

Caro smiled at him and couldn't stop a quiver from briefly crossing her lips. Sam reached out and patted her awkwardly on the shoulder. 'Room for one more hot chocolate before bed?'

※

Cracking open her eyes, Caro stretched luxuriously under the fluffy duvet. Automatically she reached for her phone before remembering that it was still buried somewhere in the depths of Bert - and the battery would be as flat as a pancake. She snuggled back, sighing with happiness at the thought of her first Christmas in a long time spent away from social media. This was already turning out to be a Christmas to remember, and it felt good to keep it all to herself.

After another stretch, Caro finally shuffled into a sitting position. She was going to have to beg Sam for the loan of a towel and a quick shower before they went down to the village for lunch - she was sure she looked like a fright.

In lieu of her phone, Caro grabbed the little alarm clock from the nightstand and peered at it.

No way! That couldn't be right, could it? Half past ten?!

Christmas morning was usually a messy mixture of her sister's overexcited children elbowing her awake at four-thirty - if she was lucky. She grimaced as the memory of last year's Christmas disaster intruded. Gareth yelling at the kids on Christmas morning. She should have dumped him on the spot rather than letting the git get all the pleasure out of doing it the next day. But she'd thought she was in love. Ha! After listening to Sam's stories of his life with Amy last night, Caro realised that she and Gareth had never been in love. Miraculously, all her sadness around that was... just gone.

Caro placed the clock down gently. What would Sam think of her, emerging this late on Christmas morning?! Mind you, it had been seriously late... or should she say early... when they'd finally headed off for bed.

She rubbed her face hard. She was knackered and in serious need of a coffee or three.

She was just about to crawl out of bed when she spotted it. How she'd missed it before, she had absolutely no idea. The biggest Christmas parcel she'd ever seen was sitting at the end of her bed, perched on the blanket chest that stood there.

She scooted down to the bottom of the bed until she was sitting in a nest of bunched-up duvet, and reached for it. Was it for her? It *had* to be for her, didn't it? It hadn't been there last night...

Blimey, it was heavy! She turned it this way and that until she spotted her name scrawled on the brown paper wrapping. Caro grinned. This was just the sort of wrapping she'd have expected from Sam. Brown parcel paper, cello-taped neatly, but strand upon strand of red, green and gold ribbon were wrapped all the way around it in every direction, the whole thing covered in little knots and bows where he'd tied them together.

Heart beating with excitement, she undid a few of the bows until she was able to slide the rest of the ribbon off the parcel. Taking a deep breath, she tore into the paper, letting it fly onto the floor on as she gasped at what was sitting there in front of her. It was the beautiful little table she'd seen in Sam's studio yesterday.

Caro let out a squeal of delight, flew out of the bed and ran down the tight staircase as fast as she could without actually breaking her neck. She ran across the empty sitting room, down the hall and into the kitchen.

Sam was standing at the Aga, a spatula in one hand and the handle of a frying pan in the other.

'Hey!' he said in surprise as she skidded into the room.

'Thank you thank you thank you!' she chanted, running over to him.

He put the pan and spatula down just in time for her to fling her arms around him in a huge bear hug.

'Whoa!' he chuckled, patting her awkwardly on the back until she relinquished her hold on him.

'Thank you - I love it - it's too much though!' she said, stepping back from him.

He grinned at her. 'I'm so glad you like it. I wanted you to have something to open for Christmas, and I saw you looking at it earlier in the day.'

'It's - it's just beautiful,' she said. 'Seriously, thank

you.' Suddenly she was feeling a little bit shy - and very aware that she was standing there in her bare feet, wearing her borrowed pyjamas.

'Breakfast?' he asked lightly, turning back to the pan.

'Ooh yes. And a bucket of coffee... but... erm, could I maybe grab a shower? And I should put some clothes on!'

'Sure, no problem! There's a pile of clean bath towels on the chair in the hall upstairs. And I agree, clothes are probably a good idea unless you want to give Alf a Christmas heart attack!' he said, shooting her a wicked smile. 'Though we'd better get a bit of a move on so that we're not late for lunch!'

She was about to head out of the room when he called her back. 'Caro - I've got another present for you by the way.'

'No. You shouldn't have!' Caro said, suddenly feeling slightly overwhelmed.

He shook his head. 'Don't get too excited. It's out by the back door. You go do your thing - breakfast will be ready in ten minutes.'

Caro headed back out into the hallway, overcome with curiosity. There, by the door, was her overnight bag. Sam had clearly been on a Christmas-morning salvage mission to see Bert.

'Bloody hero,' she smiled.

CHAPTER 12

Caro showered as quickly as possible, trying to ignore the tantalising wafts of bacon and coffee that were drifting up from the kitchen. Then, scuttling back to her bedroom wrapped in a voluminous towel, she raided her newly rescued pack. Ah the joys of her own fresh, clean clothes for Christmas day. And mascara. Heaven!

She smoothed out the folds of the vintage skater dress she had been planning to wear for Christmas at her parents' house and stared lovingly at it. Should she? Or maybe it would be a better idea to stick with the far more practical jeans and hoodie combo . . .

Sod it - she'd not spent hours adding a cute, fleece-trimmed hood and hem to the dress just to leave it languishing at home. Sure, this wasn't exactly the Christmas she'd had planned, but that didn't mean she shouldn't make an effort.

She pulled on a pair of soft wool tights and smoothed the dress down over her curves. She knew she really shouldn't blow her own trumpet, but she'd really done a good job on tailoring it so that it fitted her to perfection. She fluffed up the skirt and gave a quick, experimental spin just for the sheer joy of watching it fly out around her.

Rummaging in her bag again, she headed over to the mirror and quickly applied a slick of lip gloss and then carefully painted on a thin line of silver eyeliner. She couldn't believe it when she got the flicks right the first time. That literally never happened. A couple of sweeps of mascara and she'd be ready - there was nothing she could do about her wet hair other than give it a good rub with her towel, comb it out and hope that the warmth of the Aga would dry it before they started their walk down to the village.

Gah - the walk. She was dreading sliding her way down the hill towards the pub. With any luck, Sam would be full enough of Christmas spirit that he wouldn't mind her holding on to him most of the way down.

With one last glance at her reflection, Caro headed back down to the kitchen, her stomach rumbling in anticipation.

'Hey!' she said as she rounded the corner, only to find Sam with his back to her as he dished up two plates of sizzling fry-up.

'You were quick!' he said, bending to retrieve a plate

of bacon and black pudding he'd placed in the Aga to keep warm.

'Well - I didn't want to keep the bacon waiting,' she laughed.

'Have a seat, won't be a sec,' he said, turning to give her a quick smile. He stopped dead, staring at her.

Caro shifted her weight nervously. 'What?' she said, checking she hadn't managed to get her skirt caught in her tights.

'Oh, erm . . . nothing,' he said, his eyebrows raised in surprise. 'You just look . . . really nice.' He stopped talking and abruptly turned back to the counter to faff with their plates a bit more.

Caro raised an eyebrow. 'Thanks,' she said quietly and took a chair at the table. Had he really meant that or was that look of surprise actually one of mild embarrassment that he'd have to be seen with her in public later? She knew her sense of style was definitely not to everyone's taste.

Sam turned and placed a loaded plate in front of her.

'Are you a red or brown sauce girl?' he asked.

'Red. Ketchup all the way!' she grinned at him, all thoughts of her appearance forgotten as the smell of bacon, sausages, hash-browns and mushrooms assaulted her nose. 'Oh my goodness, we're going to explode,' she laughed, taking in the full plate as Sam handed her the bottle of ketchup from the centre of the table then proceeded to slather his own plate in brown sauce.

He grinned. 'You wait till you see the feast Lucy serves up later!'

'Shouldn't we be eating . . . I don't know . . . half a grapefruit or something and saving ourselves for later?'

Sam shook his head. 'Trust me, this is a tried and tested plan. Lucy always says lunch is served between noon and one, right?'

Caro nodded, her mouth full of runny egg and crispy white toast.

'Well, it always ends up being more like half two, three o' clock. By which time half the village are on their last legs, weak from hunger - the crisps have sold out, and the bucks fizz is having a rather amusing effect on all the empty stomachs.'

Caro snorted and realised that she was actually really excited about seeing everyone and being a part of it all. This was her weirdest Christmas to date - but, she had to admit - it was already turning out to be one of her best.

'I'm surprised it's so popular then,' Caro said when she'd swallowed her delicious mouthful.

'Are you kidding? No one in their right mind would miss out on the chance of Christmas lunch cooked by Lucy! Amy really loved it . . . she always dressed up. She'd have loved what you're wearing . . .' he trailed off looking confused for a moment.

Caro reached out and lifted her cup of coffee in a toast. 'To Amy,' she said quietly. 'Merry Christmas.'

After the smallest pause, Sam smiled at her warmly, lifted his own mug and clinked it gently against hers. 'To Amy.'

❄

It took them both a surprisingly short time to empty their plates, and they both headed into the living room to sprawl on a sofa each - a second cup of coffee in front of them.

'There's no way I'm going to be able to eat a full Christmas lunch!' laughed Caro, patting her stomach, grateful that she'd had the forethought to plan an outfit that covered a multitude of sins- as well as a multitude of meals.

'Trust me, you'll be ravenous by the time you're sitting in front of that turkey!' he grinned. 'You know, we'd better head out in a minute,' he said, glancing at his watch.

'What's the rush if she's always so late to dish up?' asked Caro in surprise.

'We've got to get one of the good seats!' said Sam. 'It was the second part of Amy's Christmas master plan. She sussed out which end of the table got first dibs on everything coming out of the kitchen,' he laughed and shook his head.

'She sounds like a woman after my own heart,' said Caro approvingly.

'You'd have loved her,' Sam said warmly. 'Everyone did.'

There was a silence between them, but it was one born of the comfort of good food and happy memories. Caro watched Sam's face as he gazed over at the Christmas tree, as it stood glittering in the morning light. A soft smile was playing on his lips and he was clearly caught up in memories of Christmas mornings gone by.

'I'll just go and grab my jacket,' said Caro, getting quietly to her feet and heading up the spiral staircase to her room.

She quickly pulled the bed into some kind of order, snagged her borrowed coat from where she'd hung it on the back of her bedroom door, and then laughed at herself. Funny how quickly it had become *her* bedroom.

That said, it was funny how quickly Sam had gone from a grumpy stranger to this warm, thoughtful friend - someone who made her laugh. Someone who had trusted her with his most precious memories. Someone who - despite the alarm bells ringing somewhere deep inside her - seemed to be thawing a part of her heart that she thought was lost under deep layers of frost. Uh oh.

Caro sat down heavily on the bed and took a deep breath. No, she shouldn't let those kind of feelings bubble up just because she was enjoying Sam's company and the fact that he was sharing so much with her. He was grieving the love of his life and she ... well, she had a lot of work to do before she was willing to become part of a "we" again.

Still, that didn't mean she couldn't enjoy Christmas with him, did it?

Pulling herself together, she got to her feet, brushed her dress down and was about to head back down the stairs when the sound of a bell ringing made her jump. Weird! That didn't sound like a door bell . . . and it sounded like it was coming from somewhere outside.

Caro hurried over to the windows and gasped. Down in the yard was possibly the last thing she'd expected to find.

There, in front of her, was - well - a sleigh. A sleigh with a chunky silver horse standing between the reins, ready to pull it. As she watched, wondering whether there had been something in her breakfast that was making her hallucinate Christmassy visions, a shortish man in a flat cap, clutching a large hand-bell came into view, closely followed by Sam. Okay, so, not a hallucination then?

'Caro?! CARO!' Sam yelled. She saw him turn back towards the cabin in search of her. She quickly ran to the stairs and navigated her way down them as fast as she could.

Running to the back door, she shoved her feet roughly into her shoe-boots and was just about to hurtle out into the yard to find out what was happening when Sam flung the door open.

'I've got a surprise for you,' he grinned.

Caro gaped at him. She wanted to tell him that she'd already spotted it, but no words came out.

Sam grabbed her hand impatiently and pulled her along the little pathway.

'No way!' she said, as they rounded into the yard. It was even better up close. The little wooden "sleigh" was actually a two-wheeled cart, painted festive red, green and gold and cleverly styled to look like a sleigh. At its front, standing patiently under an elaborate harness was the most gorgeous, chunky little horse she'd ever seen.

It wasn't particularly tall, but what it lacked in height, it more than made up for in muscle. It had a thick, curved neck and a funny, tufty mane that stuck up like a mohawk from its ears down to its back. It was a bright, gleaming silver apart from four neat, black feet, and a soft, dark nose. There was also a line of black hair down the centre of its mane, and the very tip of its fluffy white tail looked like it had been dipped in ink.

'Wow, aren't you handsome,' she cooed, taking a few steps towards the horse's head, desperate to reach out and stroke its velvety muzzle.

'Thanks very much!' came a laughing voice from just behind her.

Caro turned her head to find Alf - he of the amazing Brussel sprouts - grinning at her.

'Go on lass, Thor's a giant softy. All Fjord horses are.'

'Fjord horses?' she said.

'They're from Norway. Really friendly and brilliant in a harness like this.'

Caro turned back to the beautiful beast, who was so at ease that his eyelids were drooping. 'Hi Thor, hi gorgeous boy!' she crooned, holding out her hand to him.

Thor promptly pushed his nose into her palm and she giggled as he snuffled around, clearly looking for a treat.

'You naughty bugger,' laughed Alf. 'Here Caro, give him one of these.' The old man stepped forward and tipped a Polo mint into her palm.

The little horse's nose was twitching with interest, his velvety top lip wobbling against the side of Caro's hand as she laughed.

'You like Polos do you, Thor?' She opened her hand flat and he snaffled the mint within seconds, crunching on it with his eyes closed. Caro laughed and gently stroked his nose as she admired his beautiful harness.

'You like him then?' asked Sam, coming up beside her, a broad smile on his face.

'Like him? Have you seen Thor?! I love him!' She grinned as he began to snuffle at her hand again to see if she had any more Polos on offer.

'Well that's good,' said Sam, 'because we're not walking down to lunch!'

Caro turned to him, her eyes wide. 'You're joking?!' she breathed.

'Nope, not joking. We'll be getting a lift courtesy of Alf and Thor. You ready?' he asked, laughing at the look on her face.

She nodded, a swoop of excitement going through her.

'Come on then!' he said, taking her hand and helping her up the steps into the little carriage as Alf hopped up into the driver's seat in front of them.

Caro promptly shifted along the seat to leave plenty of room for Sam.

'Comfy?' asked Alf, turning to check on them.

'Perfect!' Sam called back to him. He grabbed a red tartan blanket from beside him and, with a flourish, settled it around both their shoulders.

'Walk on, Thor, walk on boy,' said Alf, giving the reins a jiggle.

Caro let out a little squeal of excitement as Thor started off at a gentle amble, and they made their way out of the snowy yard.

'Where are we going?' she asked in surprise as they turned right out of the yard gate instead of left down towards the village.

'We're going the scenic route,' Sam smiled at her. 'Thought you might like to see a little bit more of the village. Also, this way we can avoid poor old Thor having to deal with the steep hill!'

Caro went quiet for a moment as she watched Thor's long tail swishing in front of them as they clopped along the lane, the hedges, with their topping of fluffy snow, passing them by.

'Okay?' Sam asked gently, watching her.

'It's amazing,' she breathed. 'I can't believe you did this! Hey - was this another one of your traditions with Amy?' she asked.

Sam looked surprised and shook his head. 'Nah - as much as I think she'd have loved it if she'd tried it, Thor is quite a new addition to Alf's household!'

'So why…?'

'I just thought…' Sam paused looking slightly uncomfortable, 'I just thought you might like it. I mean, you were going to miss out on Christmas with your family - and I'd been so bloody miserable to you when we were at the craft centre - I just thought it would be a good Christmas present…'

'Good? Are you kidding? This is the best Christmas present ever.' She grinned at him and squeezed his hand. 'Thank you.'

He smiled warmly at her, gripping her fingers tightly in his before promptly letting go and turning to stare out of his side of the carriage.

They passed a farmhouse set back from the road, its thatched roof still wearing a cap of snow - a ribbon of smoke trailing out of the chimney into the cold,

Christmas morning air. Caro smiled as she watched a scattering of brown hens scratching in the snow on the front lawn as they trundled by.

Alf pulled Thor to a halt at a junction and waited for a large, four-wheel-drive to drive slowly past before he allowed the horse to amble out. Caro grinned and waved when she spotted two little kids waving at them from the back window as the vehicle disappeared off ahead of them.

'You know, I don't think I want to go anywhere in a car ever again,' she said. 'This has got to be the only way to travel. How attached do you reckon Alf is to Thor? I'm sure he wouldn't mind living in a third floor flat in Plymouth - what do you think?'

Sam laughed. 'Depends on how many boxes of Polos you've got in the flat. I think Alf's pretty smitten though!' He pulled the blanket up again so that it covered them properly, then leaned into her so that his shoulder nudged hers.

'What?' she said, turning her shining eyes on him.

'Thank you!'

'What are you thanking me for, you idiot? You're the one who's literally taking me on a Christmas sleigh ride right now!'

Sam shrugged. 'I know. But, thank you - I didn't think I'd ever enjoy Christmas again - but having you here... well, I'm having fun.'

Caro smiled at him as a warm ball of happiness lodged itself in her stomach. 'Me too, Sam. Me too.'

CHAPTER 13

'Nearly there Thor, come on now lad,' cried Alf. The little horse had suddenly slowed to peer curiously in through the front window of one of the cottages they were passing as they made their way towards the pub.

It had been one of the most magical journeys Caro had ever been on. They'd ambled down from the higher roads and into the village following a circuitous route. Thor had made very light work of pulling the carriage through the snow.

The village looked glorious from her perch, and as she sat, snug and warm under the blanket with Sam at her side, Caro wished for a moment that this little trip didn't have to come to an end - both the sleigh ride and her stay in Little Bamton. She could feel that she was falling in love with this place.

The snow still lay in a thick blanket over everything. They hadn't yet had any more since the first heavy fall, but the pearly-grey clouds and strange silence made Caro think that more snow would arrive before the day was over.

The cottages looked even prettier now that she could admire them from under the twinkling white lights that had been strung between the old-fashioned lampposts. Caro loved being able to peep into the lighted windows as they rode past, catching tiny glimpses of families enjoying their Christmas morning rituals while the world outside waited, calm and quiet under its blanket of snow.

How very different this was to the Christmas morning she'd been expecting. A pang of sadness hit Caro as she thought of her mum and dad. She'd been so looking forward to celebrating with them - and her sister and nephews - but now she was on her way to have Christmas lunch with a group of strangers.

'Hey, you doing okay?' Sam asked quietly, his cheeks flushed with the cold and his eyes sparkling as they reflected the lights above them.

The concern on his face melted her moment of sadness in seconds. What had she been thinking? She wasn't off for lunch with strangers at all - she was spending Christmas with friends. Special friends, even if they were brand new. And this particular friend had just made a dream come true for the six-year-old little girl inside her. She was literally dashing through the snow in a one-horse open sleigh. Okay, maybe not *dashing* - and maybe not quite a sleigh - but near enough.

'I'm . . . perfect. This is incredible. Thank you so much, Sam.'

Sam smiled at her bashfully and bumped her shoulder with his. 'My pleasure.'

'Whoa Thor. Whoa lad!' cried Alf as they drew up in front of the pub.

'Awww!' said Caro, and Sam smirked at her before climbing down. He turned and reached out to give her a steady hand as she climbed reluctantly down from the carriage.

'Can I say goodbye to Thor?' she said.

'Of course, it's only polite!' said Sam, his face serious though his eyes were still twinkling.

Caro walked up to Thor's handsome head and held out her hand for him to sniff, then reached up to scratch under his fluffy fringe. 'Thank you Thor, you're amazing - you beautiful boy,' she said.

'Now then lass, you know he won't let you get away without a couple of these,' said Alf, coming to stand next to her, waving half a packet of Polos.

Caro grinned as she helped herself to a couple and fed them, one at a time, to a very enthusiastic Thor.

'Thank you so much, Alf!' she said, turning to the old man, and then, before he could say anything in return, she threw her arms around him and pulled him into a warm hug, planting a kiss on his cheek.

'Pleasure, lass. Merry Christmas!' he said when she

finally let go of him. He took a step back from her, his cheeks flaming red, a surprised smile on his face.

'Oh, are you not coming in for lunch?!' she asked. Surely he hadn't come all the way down here just for them?

'Aye lass, I'll be in presently. Thor's not too welcome in the bar though, so I'll take him around the back for a bit of a rest and some nice hay while we eat.'

'Brilliant,' she said, 'see you in there. And thank you! Bye Thor!' she said, patting him again.

'See you in a minute, Alf!' said Sam as he started to lead Caro towards the door of the pub.

'Aye lad. You've got a good lass there,' he nodded at Caro approvingly.

'Oh she isn't-' Sam started.

'He isn't-' said Caro, cutting across him.

Alf disappeared around the corner with Thor and the empty carriage.

Caro glanced up at Sam, feeling slightly awkward.

'Come on,' he said after clearing his throat, 'let's go face the music.'

'What do you mean?' asked Caro in surprise.

He nodded his head towards one of the pub windows and, following his gaze, she spotted Lucy, Sue, the vicar and a couple of other faces she recognised from the previous night peering out at them.

'Looks like we've been rumbled,' Caro laughed.

She followed Sam inside, and the wave of babbling voices that washed over her sounded extra loud after their peaceful journey through the village in the quiet morning air.

As she closed the door and came to stand beside Sam, complete silence descended.

Oh. My. Giddy. Aunts.

It felt like the entire village was already here and every single one of them had stopped talking to turn and stare at her and Sam.

Caro's cheeks flamed yet again, and she knew that it wasn't entirely due to the warmth of the roaring open fire at the other end of the bar.

'Hello you two!' cried Lucy in greeting, breaking the strange moment with her customary cheer. She bustled over to Caro from her spot beside the window, and without so much as a blush about the fact that she'd been spying on the two of them just seconds before, she pulled Caro into a bear hug, before letting go and repeating the action with Sam.

'Happy Christmas,' she said warmly. 'Did you enjoy your ride, Caro?'

'So much,' she said, unable to stop a massive smile spreading across her face. 'I'm trying to figure out if Alf will let me take Thor home with me!'

'Do that and there will be quite a few broken hearts left behind him. That horse is one of the village's most beloved residents!' she said.

'I can see why - he's gorgeous.'

'Drinks?' Lucy asked, leading them towards the bar.

The small crowd made way for her and Sam as Lucy scooted in behind to serve them.

'I'll have glass of red, if that's okay?' she asked.

'Of course, my love. Pint of the usual Sam?'

Sam nodded gratefully.

'Erm, Lucy - how come you're running the bar and cooking and serving and . . . everything, all at the same time?' asked Caro, stripping her coat off as the heat started to make her feel like she was coming to the boil.

'Ah - well, I'm a bit short staffed. Tracey, my main barmaid, moved away at the beginning of December - that's why the flat upstairs was available for Sue's family to stay - it goes with the job.

'Anyway, I can't ask any of the others to work on Christmas Day just because I love feeding the hordes! They've already been doing more than their fair share to cover Tracey's hours.'

'But you can't do it all on your own!' Caro said horrified.

'Don't worry about that, I'll manage. I've got Sue helping out in the kitchen.'

'When she's not spying on us arriving!' said Caro mischievously.

'Oh, you spotted us then?!' said Lucy looking slightly shamefaced.

'Yup,' said Sam rolling his eyes good-naturedly.

'Well, it is quite a sight to behold on Christmas day, you know. And - I hope you don't mind me saying - it's so lovely to see you looking so happy love. Actually, that goes for both of you!'

'Thanks Luce,' Sam muttered.

Caro could feel waves of awkwardness suddenly start to emanate from him.

He took his pint with a grunt of thanks, then promptly popped it down on the bar. 'I'm just going to head out back and check Alf's doing okay with Thor. Back in a minute.'

He disappeared through the crowd before either of them had the chance to say anything.

'Crap - sorry love. I didn't mean to embarrass him,' said Lucy, handing her a glass of wine, worry clouding her usually cheerful face.

Caro shook her head. 'I'm sure you didn't - I think it's just a lot for him to take. I rather wrecked his plans for a quiet Christmas.' She smiled warmly at Lucy, and then decided to change the subject.

'So . . . how do you fancy an extra pair of helping hands?' she asked Lucy, who was gulping at a glass of water while she had the chance.

'Nope. No way, I can't ask you to do that. You're here to enjoy yourself.'

'You didn't ask. And anyway, I love working behind bars - I did it all the way through uni so I know my way around.'

Lucy shook her head. 'It's Christmas!'

'Don't you trust me?' Caro pouted, a twinkle in her eye.

'Of course I do!' Lucy laughed, still shaking her head.

'Luce!' called one of the guys from the group behind Caro, 'six pints of Guinness, two red wines and a sherry for Uncle Dave, please.'

Lucy stared at Caro for just a couple of seconds and then with a quick flick of her head, she beckoned for her to join her behind the bar. 'You're on!' she laughed.

❄

'What on earth?!' laughed Sam when he reappeared from the back of the pub fifteen minutes later only to find Caro manning the bar on her own. She had a huge grin on her face as she flirted with the locals, pulled pints and doled out sherry left right and centre. 'How long was I gone for?!'

'Lucy was looking a bit busy so I offered to help,' said Caro, taking advantage of a momentary lull to sip her wine.

'And she let you? I think you've probably broken some kind of record there.'

'Just good timing, I think,' said Caro. 'Anyway - I reckon lunch should be ready soon, don't you?'

'Don't forget what I told you!' said Sam, shaking his head.

'Can we get some crisps over here please love?' a little old lady named Violet called from the other end of the bar.

Caro caught Sam's eye and they grinned at each other before she hurried over to help.

'Alf and Thor okay?' she asked once she'd handed out three packets from the fast-dwindling stash of salt and vinegar crisps.

'Fine,' said Sam. 'Sorry about abandoning you - this place can be . . .'

'A lot to take?' Caro laughed, finishing his sentence.

'Nailed it,' he said, raising a rueful eyebrow.

❄

Caro clutched her stomach tenderly as Sue got to her feet and chimed a knife against her wine glass to get everyone's attention. They were all taking a much-needed break between the main course and pudding. Caro already felt like she was going to explode.

'Three cheers for Lucy!' Sue yelled without any preamble. The entire pub erupted with cheers and applause. Happy faces, flushed with good food, grinned at Lucy as she got to her feet and hugged Sue, kissing her on the cheek.

'Merry Christmas everyone,' Lucy said, smiling around at what must have been the entire village - plus all the added extra people who'd found themselves stranded here because of the snow. They were all piled in - every single table in the place had been dragged together to form one giant, snaking dining table that ran the entire length of the bar and wrapped around both ends.

Lucy went to stand behind the bar so that everyone could see her, no matter where they were perched.

'I just wanted to say thank you for coming and celebrating Christmas here with me. This is the absolute highlight of my year. Thank you.'

There was another round of cheering, and Lucy wiped a stray tear from the corner of her eye as she waited for them to calm down again, her green paper party hat sitting at a jaunty angle on her curls.

'There are a few people I'd like to thank for making this happen. As ever, lovely Sue for all her friendship, help and support in tackling the sprout mountain!'

Everyone cheered and Caro, who was sitting next to Sue, gave her a one-armed squeeze.

'On the topic of sprouts - and in fact, most of the delicious veggies that we've just pigged-out on - a massive thank you to everyone over at the allotments for all your hard work growing this year's Christmas dinner - especially Alf!'

There were cheers around the room and Alf stood up to take a little bow.

'Also, Alf wanted me to tell you that Thor's here, and he'll be happy to do little sleigh rides around the village for the rest of the afternoon if anyone would like to!'

At this, the children in attendance went wild,

squealing to each other in delight and begging their parents to be allowed a ride after dinner.

'Okay - I'm not going to keep you much longer - just two more to go. I want to say a big thanks - on behalf of all of us - to Sam for donating our beautiful Christmas tree again this year.'

Caro turned to Sam, who was sitting on her other side, and watched as he turned a beautiful shade of cranberry as he raised a hand awkwardly to acknowledge the applause.

'And finally,' shouted Lucy, 'most of you will have met Caro by now!'

Caro turned away from Sam and looked up at Lucy in surprise.

'She really is our Christmas angel. She wasn't expecting to be spending Christmas in Little Bamton, but we are so lucky to have her here with us. Not only did she help us conquer the sprout mountain, she single-handedly wrestled with the carrots, and then, on top of all that - took over today's bar duties ... which is why lunch wasn't *quite* as late as usual. So - three cheers for Caro!'

Everyone cheered and Caro didn't know where to look. She really hadn't expected that - she didn't need them to say thank you - she'd just wanted to help out and be a part of things.

Much to her surprise, she could feel waves of giggles coming from Sam as the clapping started to die away.

'What?' she hissed at him

'The look on your face!' he spluttered.

Caro stuck her tongue out at him. 'Be quiet and eat your pudding,' she chuckled, as Sue handed down a steaming bowl of Christmas pud, followed by a jug of cream.

'So, all that's left for me to do is make a toast,' said Lucy, her voice turning serious as she raised her glass. 'Here's to our loved ones on Christmas Day - wherever they may be. Merry Christmas.'

CHAPTER 14

'Urrrggghhh!' Caro groaned, leaning back in her chair.

'I second that!' sighed Sam, reaching out and picking up his coffee cup as if to take a sip, only to replace it without bringing it to his mouth. 'I'm never eating again,' he whimpered.

'Urrrrrgh!' Caro agreed.

'Thirds?' asked Sue, waving a plate with half a rich, moist Christmas pudding under her nose, a slightly evil gleam in her eye.

'Get that away from me,' laughed Caro, fighting to sit upright in her chair.

Sue chuckled and got to her feet to start clearing the leftovers off the table.

The bar had emptied out considerably now that most people had finished picking at their extra helpings of pudding. Caro had felt bad as she'd watched

Lucy and Sue start to clear the table- but Lucy had assured her that there was no way she was doing any more than moving everything into the kitchen for now.

'I think,' said Sam, rubbing his face, 'I need some fresh air. I need to be upright to give lunch the chance to sink.'

'Urgh,' said Caro, the thought of even moving right now was more than she could handle. But then, fresh air was quite tempting. It was warm and stuffy in the bar. 'It's either that or a nap,' she said as he got to his feet and stretched.

'Come on,' he held his hand out to her and she reluctantly allowed him to pull her to her feet with a groan. 'Grab your coat!'

'No way will I be needing that,' she said, fanning her face, which was flushed with too much good food and drink.

'Trust me - you will!'

Caro grabbed it from the back of her chair and turned to Sue and Lucy who were standing behind the bar, whispering to each other and giggling. She smiled as a bloom of warmth spread through her chest. This should have been a rubbish day - eating Christmas lunch surrounded by strangers. Instead she'd found herself at home, in the company of people who already felt like family.

'You off, love?' called Sue in surprise, seeing her reluctantly pulling on her borrowed coat.

Caro shook her head. 'Don't worry - we'll be back to help you sort this lot out in a little while - Sam and I are just going out for a walk. I need some fresh air before you have to make a bed up for me in front of the fire!'

'Enjoy. No rush - this lot'll keep,' chuckled Lucy, throwing one arm around Sue's shoulders and picking up her glass of wine with the other.

'Thanks for a gorgeous lunch, Luce,' Sam called from the door.

'My pleasure. Now you two behave yourselves!' she giggled, wiggling her eyebrows.

Sam let out a sigh and shook his head in amusement, and Caro ushered him through the door before the pair of them could say anything else that might have a bad effect on his relaxed, cheerful mood.

As soon as she stepped out into the snowy square, Caro felt better. She drew the cold, crisp air deep into her lungs and felt her post-lunch drowsiness start to drift away. She raised her face to the sky, looking up through the glimmering strands of Christmas lights to the clouds, which even now seemed to be darkening in preparation for the next snowstorm. It might be a day late, but it looked like it was on its way after all.

Just then, the sound of light, tinkling bells drew her attention back to ground level, and Thor came jogging back into the square with Alf riding behind him, the carriage empty.

Sam came to stand next to her as they watched a

young family appear through the door of the pub behind them, the three little kids practically bouncing with excitement.

'Ready for yer ride home?' he called to them, as they cheered and whooped, scrambling up into the back of the carriage, followed more slowly by their clearly exhausted parents.

Alf waited until they were all settled and then encouraged Thor into a gentle plod as they turned around and headed back towards the village.

'Merry Christmas!' shouted the kids out of the back.

Both Sam and Caro called back to them, Caro waving madly until they disappeared around the gentle bend in the road - though in reality, she was actually waving to Thor rather than the kids.

'Where do you fancy going?' asked Sam, turning to her with a smile.

'Are we allowed to go and look at the allotments?' she asked. 'Sue told me so much about them and how much everyone enjoys working up there.'

'Of course!' Said Sam. 'Though there won't be much to see at this time of year.'

Caro shrugged. 'I don't mind. I'd just like to see them so I can picture it all when . . . when I'm back home,' she trailed off with a sad sigh.

Sam raised his eyebrows, clearly picking up on her momentary slump.

'What's up?' he asked as they set off across the

snowy square, heading for the little lane between the vicarage and the craft centre.

'I'm just being silly,' said Caro shrugging, flashing him a small, embarrassed smile.

'Tell me anyway,' he said, grabbing her elbow as she skidded slightly on the compacted snow where Thor had trodden it all in.

'I've just had the best Christmas here,' she said.

Sam chuckled. 'Not quite the one you were expecting though?'

'Definitely not. Even better I think, and one hundred percent better than last year.'

Sam made a sound in his throat, and Caro suddenly stopped to stare at him in horror. 'Oh Sam, I'm such an idiot. It was nothing ... let's talk about something else.'

'No, don't apologise,' he said, looking surprised. 'I've told you so much about me, and you've listened. It's my turn. What happened?' he asked curiously.

'My ex,' she said, her face glum, cross with herself now for even mentioning it at all and letting that idiot intrude on her wonderful Christmas day.

'Oh . . . there's an ex?' he asked lightly, leading her into the little lane.

'Yep. Put it like this - he wasn't an ex on Christmas Day but he was by the end of Boxing Day.'

'Uh oh, that sounds pretty shitty,' said Sam, casting a glance at her. 'Was it you or him who ended it?'

'Him,' said Caro, pulling a face. 'Though he behaved

like such an obnoxious git to my whole family on Christmas day, I should have got in there first.'

'Why didn't you?'

Caro paused a moment. Reaching out she yanked a bare piece of dead grass out of the hedgerow and proceeded to snap it into little bits.

'I didn't want to make a scene, I guess - though he was already doing that. I mean, who's horrible to little kids on Christmas day? He had both of my nephews in tears!'

'Sounds like a real charmer,' muttered Sam.

'Yeah, well,' she huffed, feeling her anger at Gareth - which was always boiling just under the surface - flare up.

'So you can't have been that sorry when he ended things?' prompted Sam.

'There's always more to it than just losing that one person from your life though, isn't there?' she sighed.

Sam nodded, recognition clear on his face.

'I mean - I know this is nothing compared to what you've been through,' she said quickly.

'It's not a competition,' he said seriously, pausing at a huge wooden gate - patches of blue, flaking paint showing through here and there beneath the snow. He drew a loop of bailer-twine over the top of a post that was set into the hedge and, lifting the gate slightly, managed to open it wide enough for them to sidle through sideways. 'I do know what you mean though - you lose joint friends, extended family . . .'

'Our home together,' Caro added, nodding.

'Nightmare,' sighed Sam, sympathy evident in his voice.

'It was. I mean, it sounds really trivial, but I'd been getting ready to launch my own business and give up my job - and suddenly I had to pay for a house move I wasn't expecting and fork out for a place on my own.'

'And your business?' asked Sam, turning to close the gate behind them.

'I couldn't afford to go ahead with it. It's all been on the back burner. I've had a whole extra year working in that bloody shop, but no matter how hard I work, how many hours I put in, I just can't build up the buffer I need before setting out on my own.'

She sighed and ran her hand over the top of one of the fence posts, pushing the little pile of snow to the ground with a soft *flump*.

'You know, if I can be of any help - you can call me. I mean, I can't do much - but I've built my design business up from it just being me working alone to having a team of a dozen guys working for me. And I managed to keep it afloat when I lost Amy - that was probably the biggest challenge. I've figured a few things out along the way, and if picking my brains could help you - even a little bit - well, I'd be happy to help.'

'Thank you,' said Caro, touched by the sincerity in his voice. 'You know, I might take you up on that.'

She followed him as he wound his way a little further along the path until it came to an opening.

'Here we are. The allotments. If Lucy's place is like the village indoor living room - then this is the outdoor equivalent!' he laughed.

Caro gazed around at the huge space - which was basically a paddock that had been turned into several little growing plots. Pretty much everything was covered in snow, but she admired the bare stalks of what must have been the Brussels sprout crop lying beside the path.

Towards the back of the space were several massive compost heaps, their sides constructed from old wooden delivery pallets.

'Wow, this is serious!' she said.

'Yep - everyone brings their compost bins down here to empty. You see how there are three stacks? There's always one that's open for new scraps, one that's full and covered over, doing its thing, and a third that remains empty, ready for the others to be turned over into to keep the compost working.'

'How on earth do you know all that?' laughed Caro, dragging him over for a closer look.

'If you live here, you know how the compost system works!' he laughed.

There were also two small but perfectly formed polly-tunnels to one side of the space, and Sam explained that they were used to produce strawberries for the Summer Fete as well as enough salad to keep the entire village going.

Caro stomped her cold feet to warm them up a bit and blew into her hands.

'Had enough?' he asked.

'Maybe for today,' she laughed.

He nodded and led the way back down the path. 'You'll have to come back when the sun's out - there's a lot more to see up here when it's not completely covered in snow.'

'I'd really like that!' she said softly.

They both fell silent, deep in thought.

'So,' said Sam finally, 'what's next?'

Caro turned to him, a look of mild surprise on her face. 'A cuppa, then help Lucy tidy up and then - did I hear someone say that there's a carol service in the Church at five?' Why was he asking her? He was more likely to know the details than she was, surely?

Sam laughed. 'Well yes, that all sounds about right . . . but I actually meant for you . . . more generally . . . and your business.'

Caro shrugged. 'Mum and dad's place tomorrow if the roads are clear - and then back to work, I guess. Like I said - the business idea's on the back burner - and that's probably where it'll stay . . . although . . .'

'Although-?' Sam prodded, curiously.

They both paused as they reached the edge of the square.

'Well - these last few days here with you have changed something,' she said slowly.

'In what way?' asked Sam, looking surprised.

'It's made me think that - even though things might not be following the original plan - maybe they can work another way.'

'Deep!' he laughed.

Caro gave him a prod with her elbow. 'Oi, I'm being serious. This wasn't the Christmas I had planned, the one I'd been looking forward to for ages - but I'm having the most amazing time. And I wouldn't be here if things hadn't gone "wrong",' she said, making air quotes around the last word. 'It's just reminded me that there's a whole world out here to explore, and I don't have to stick to what I know, just because I feel like I have to. There are other ways of doing things.'

'Now, that sounds exciting. Anything specific brewing?' he asked.

Caro shrugged. Yes, there was - but it felt so new, so fresh and delicate, that she found she didn't want to jinx it by saying it out loud yet.

'Watch this space,' she said with a smile. 'Now then - what about the more immediate "next"?' she asked, turning to Sam and very deliberately changing the subject.

'Well,' said Sam, 'there's something I've been wanting to do since the first night I helped you back to my place in the snow,' he said smiling.

Caro fought hard to stop her mouth from dropping open. Her eyes widened and she was convinced her heartbeat could be heard across the entire square. Did he mean what she thought he meant?

She watched as he turned away from her briefly, and a look of confusion drifted across her face momentarily before-

'YOU LITTLE- !!!' she squealed as a giant snowball hit her square on the shoulder, the icy powder spraying up onto her neck and face. She shook her herself, trying to dislodge the cold, wet mess.

Sam was doubled over, pink in the face with laughter as he watched the shock on Caro's face turn into a look of gleeful determination.

'This means war,' she growled, scooping up her own handful and lobbing it at him.

CHAPTER 15

The next twenty minutes were spent in pure, joyful chaos. What started out as a couple of jokey snowballs thrown at each other quickly escalated into an all-out village-wide battle. More and more people joined them in the square as they came to find out what all the laughter and squealing was about.

Lucy and Sue promptly joined forces with Caro - but things were evened up when Alf re-appeared having taken Thor back home for his tea. Alf proved a surprisingly good shot and had them all running for cover in seconds. Then, all of Sue's extended family joined in. Even the vicar appeared and rolled his sleeves up, much to Caro's delight and secret respect. The fight quickly spread from the square, down the road into people's front gardens, and round the back of the pub into the car park.

Finally, exhausted, soaked, and simultaneously

boiling hot from all the running around and freezing cold from being covered from head-to-toe in snowy slush, a truce was called and they all trooped back to the pub.

Lucy headed straight upstairs and quickly reappeared with a washing basket full to the brim with dozens of warm, fluffy towels and started handing them out.

Once again, the bar was full of the warm buzz of chatter as they all towelled their hair dry and peeled off sodden coats, scarves and gloves to hang them as close to the open fire as they could.

'I'd take those shoes off, Caro love!' said Lucy, looking down at her drenched feet.

'Oh no, I'm so sorry,' said Caro guiltily, looking around at the mess they'd all made of the floor.

'Don't be silly,' laughed Lucy, 'I just don't want you catching a cold. Here!' She handed Caro a long, thick pair of warm socks that had a non-slip bottom to them. 'Get these on, shove some newspaper inside your shoes and pop them over by the fire!'

'You think of everything - thank you Lucy!' said Caro, pulling her into a slightly damp hug.

'My pleasure,' said Lucy, beaming. 'You can borrow a pair of wellies for later too - I've gathered a collection of pretty much every size available over the years!'

As soon as she had dried off and warmed up a bit, Caro helped Lucy and Sue hand out hot chocolate and mulled wine to warm everyone up, while Sam headed out into the kitchen to make a start on taming the chaos that was the aftermath of Christmas lunch.

'Need a hand?' Caro asked. As soon as she'd finished helping Lucy, she'd headed out to rescue him from the piles of dirty dishes.

'Nope. Both the machines are loaded and on, I've got all the pans soaking and the leftovers are wrapped up and in the fridge. I think that's as far as we can go until we can do a second couple of dishwasher loads later.'

'Good job,' grinned Caro, holding her hand up for a high five, which Sam returned with a delighted look on his face.

'Hey Caro?' he said, catching her hand to stop her turning away from him, a smile still tugging at the corner of his mouth.

'Yeah?' she said, her heart doing that ridiculous drumming thing again. She really had to get a grip. All this Christmas cheer combined with Sam's beautiful, twinkling eyes staring down at her was making her feel quite giddy.

'Have I said thank you?' he said quietly, not taking his eyes off hers. Caro nodded, but he carried on anyway.

'Thank you for reminding me how to have fun,' he said. 'Thank you for making me feel like that's okay.'

'I didn't . . . I mean, I . . .' she stuttered.

He shook his head, a soft smile on his face. 'Not great at taking a compliment, are you?'

Caro shrugged. 'You're the one that did it.'

'Yes - but you're the one who helped me.'

Caro couldn't look away from him, even though they'd both stopped talking. Her ears were filled with the rhythmic hum coming from the dishwashers and the sounds of laughter drifting through from the bar.

The space between the two of them started to disappear as they leaned towards each other.

'How're you both getting on in here . . . OH! Sorry, sorry!' Sue squeaked.

Caro and Sam jumped apart as if they'd been electrified.

'We're fine!'

'All sorted!'

They both gabbled over the top of each other as Sue looked from one to the other and then started reversing back towards the bar.

'I'll just leave you two in peace,' she said, breaking into a naughty grin as she scooted away, no doubt in urgent search of Lucy.

Sam cleared his throat and started to move pans aimlessly around on the worktop. The moment had *definitely* passed.

'I'll just . . .'

'We should . . .'

They both stopped and started to laugh. Sam turned, pink cheeked, back to Caro. 'That was . . .'

'Yeah!' Caro smiled.

'How about we head back out and grab another mulled wine before that lot drink Lucy dry?' he said.

Caro nodded. 'Are you up for going to the carol service or have you had enough?' she crossed her fingers behind her back, hoping that whatever had happened just now hadn't ruined the lovely day they'd been sharing.

'You know, I think a bit of singing is just what we need to finish the day off in style, don't you?'

Caro grinned at him. 'Absolutely.'

※

The little church looked so different this evening to when Caro had been in there on Christmas Eve. The whole place was lit by the soft glow of candlelight, the lamps on the walls were turned low, just adding a golden warmth to the old stone walls.

As the organist launched into the opening bars of O Come All Ye Faithful and Caro got to her feet with the rest of the village, she could feel the hairs on the backs of her arms prickle. This, right here, was exactly what people meant when they talked about the magic of Christmas.

She grinned as she heard Sam's angry-bumblebee voice take up the opening line, and quickly added her own voice to the song.

On her other side stood Lucy, and as their combined voices belted out the final *Oh come let us adore him*, she felt Lucy take hold of her hand and give it a little squeeze.

Caro turned and smiled at her as they finished the song, squeezing her new friend's hand in return. Meeting these wonderful people was definitely the most unexpected gift she'd ever received - and that was saying something after the table and the sleigh ride!

'Before we have our last carol of the evening,' said the vicar in his ringing tones as they all settled back onto the pews, 'I would like us all to take a moment to remember our families, friends and loved ones who are not here with us to celebrate Christmas this year. Time, geography and, of course, the last great journey can come between us. But on Christmas day, if we open our hearts, we can feel their love reaching out to us across that distance, just as they can feel ours. And so, let us all take a moment to send and receive that love - that Christmas magic we all have in us.'

Caro blinked hard and tried to swallow the lump that had formed in her throat. She gazed hard at the floor until Lucy gave her hand another little squeeze.

She peeped up at her friend who gave her a friendly smile, and nodded across at Sam. Caro followed her gaze and felt her heart squeeze as she spotted a tear making its way down his cheek.

Without thinking about it, Caro reached across with her free hand and laced her fingers through his. She felt Sam go completely stiff for just a moment before his hand softened in hers and he took a firmer grip on it, shooting her a grateful smile before quickly wiping at his cheeks with his other hand.

Thankfully, the final carol was another belter, and as they all got to their feet for one last time to sing Ding Dong Merrily on High, Caro poured all her pent-up emotion into the song. By the end of the last long *gloria*, sang at the top of their voices - she was beaming and so was Sam.

He reached his arm around her shoulders and squeezed her to him for the briefest second, before letting go and filing out of the church with rest of the village.

As Sam was swept away from her back down the aisle with the chattering crowd, she felt her heart plummet for the briefest moment. It was nearly all over. This gorgeous little Christmas bubble - where she'd been so unbelievable happy - would soon be nothing more than a wonderful memory.

Her heart squeezed as the emotion of the day, combined with her sadness at having to leave everyone here at Little Bamton behind, brought tears to her eyes.

'What's the verdict then, Caro? Did we do Christmas proud after all?' asked Sue, coming up behind her and squeezing her shoulder.

Caro quickly blinked away her tears before Sue could spot them and nodded. 'And then some!' she said, her voice feeling hot and thick in her throat.

'You and Sam coming back for one last Christmas

drink with me and Lucy before heading home?' she asked.

'I reckon that sounds like the perfect plan,' replied Caro, wrapping her arm around Sue's shoulders just as Lucy took her other hand, and the three of them made their way out of the church together.

They were half way across the square when Caro realised that she'd left her borrowed coat folded under the pew back in the church.

'Ah, don't worry about that, love!' said Lucy, clearly keen to get back home and put her feet up. 'I can easily pick that up any old time.

'It's okay - I'll nip back for it now. Sam and I are walking home, so as long as you don't mind, I could do with keeping hold of it for one more night anyway, if that's okay?'

'Of course, love. Do you want us to come back with you?'

Caro shook her head. 'No, you guys carry on - I won't be a moment.' She turned and made her way back through the few stragglers who had stopped for a chat on the far side of the square.

'Merry Christmas Caro!'

'Thanks Caro!'

'Happy Christmas!'

Every single person she passed greeted her like an old friend, and her heart sang as she made her way into the church and back down the now-empty aisle.

Turning back into their pew, she ducked down and

retrieved the coat from where she'd left it. Shaking it out, she pulled it on and gazed around the beautiful little church for one last time.

Then, keen to get back to the others, she hurried towards the door and ran full pelt into someone coming the other way.

'Oomph!' she grunted. 'Sorry, I'm so sorry . . . oh, hi Sam!' she said in surprise.

'Hey! You okay?' he asked, steadying her with a hand on each shoulder.

Caro nodded and smiled up at him. 'I thought you were back at the pub?' she said.

'Lucy said you'd left your coat behind, so I was coming to get it for you...'

'Done,' Caro grinned. 'I was just taking a last look around - it's so beautiful in here,' she said, conscious that Sam's hands were still gently resting on her shoulders. 'And all the amazing candles and greenery they've used to decorate the place...' She was babbling now and she knew it, but suddenly here they were - back in this moment again. And this time there were no dishwashers running in the background . . . and no Sue to interrupt them.

'See,' she said, unable to stop herself, and pointed over their heads at a bunch of strategically placed greenery.

Sam raised an amused eyebrow at her before glancing up too.

'Huh,' he said, 'mistletoe.'

'Oh,' said Caro.

'Indeed,' said Sam, dropping his eyes back to hers.

Caro swallowed, and then - before anyone could sneak up on them and ruin this perfect moment - she raised herself on her tiptoes and gently brushed her lips against his.

Sam froze for the briefest moment before wrapping his arms around her and pulling her in closer.

CHAPTER 16

Caro stayed stock still under the duvet. She didn't want to open her eyes. She didn't want it all to be over yet. She smiled to herself and snuggled down into the warmth, determined to relive some of the gorgeous moments of the day-before before they faded in her memory: Thor's velvety nose snuffling into her hand for more polos; the comfort of the fire as she'd stuffed herself with multiple helpings of pudding; the warmth of friendship that had tingled through her as Lucy had reached over to hold her hand in church; the unexpected softness of that kiss under the mistletoe.

That kiss. That perfect kiss. It had been the best, most unexpected Christmas Day she'd ever had. And now it was over.

The morning light was flooding in through the glass front of her cabin bedroom, filtering through her closed eyelids and demanding that she get out of bed and greet the new day. All Caro wanted to do was stay in her warm, Christmas bubble. Real life was starting to feel far too close for comfort.

After their moment under the mistletoe last night, Sam had offered her his arm and they'd both returned to the pub for another mulled wine with Sue and Lucy. With the curious gaze of their two friends on them, they'd done nothing more than share the odd, secret look, neither of them wanting to become the talk of the entire village from now until the New Year.

Eventually, Sue had offered them a lift back up the hill in her truck - claiming that she wouldn't be able to settle until she knew that they were home safe. Sam had accepted gratefully - much to Caro's relief given how warm and full she was feeling - but she couldn't help but feel a little bit disappointed at the same time. A romantic stroll home in the dark might have been the perfect end to the day.

As they'd both waved Sue off and turned their backs on the snowy yard to sit by the wood-burner, the magic of the day already seemed to be slipping away. Caro had wanted nothing more than to curl up on the sofa next to Sam and hear more stories about village life, but instead he'd placed her mug of hot chocolate carefully in front of her and then retreated to sit on the other sofa.

They'd made polite conversation as they drank,

shared an awkward goodnight hug and then headed off to their separate rooms.

Caro let out a huge sigh, finally opened her eyes and threw the duvet off her. There was no point lounging around in bed - it was time to get back to reality. It was probably a good thing that nothing more had happened between them - and if she kept telling herself that, she might actually start to believe it.

She snuck quietly to the bathroom, washed and dressed quickly and then ran down to the kitchen. No matter how strange and stilted things had become between them last night, Caro couldn't wait to see Sam again. She knew her heart was in serious danger right now - but she simply didn't care. She didn't have much longer here with him, and she wasn't going to waste it being all quiet and awkward.

Caro bounded around the corner into the kitchen. Sam turned to her, his face going from a look of surprise to a huge, warm grin, to awkward confusion in such quick succession that it was as much as she could do not to laugh.

'Erm, hi!' he said, his features finally settling into a sweet, genuine smile.

'Morning!' she said, returning his smile ten-fold.

'Tea?' he asked, turning back to the kettle, clearly glad to have something to do while he composed himself.

'Please,' she said, and wandering over, she came to stand right next to him.

She watched as Sam spooned tea leaves into a little brown and cream striped pot before glancing down at her. 'Erm, hi?' he said, looking confused again.

'Hi,' she said, a warm wave crashing through her as his dark eyes met hers. Caro lent in and playfully bumped her arm against his, beaming at him. She couldn't look away, and from the look of bemused panic on his face, he was having the same issue.

'Sam - thank you,' she said. 'For yesterday.'

He returned her smile again. 'Same,' he said. 'I'm sorry about last night.'

Caro shook her head, opening her mouth to tell him not to be silly, but he continued before she could get the words out.

'Getting back here . . . I don't know . . . sobered me up a bit.'

'I get it,' she said, taking a small step away from him, her heart sinking a little bit. 'We'd all had a lot to eat and drink and . . .'

'No,' said Sam quickly, finally putting the teaspoon down and turning to face her properly. 'No, I didn't mean sober in that way. Just, getting back here, there was a massive dose of real life - or . . . life *before* . . . to deal with. Life with Amy,' he sighed.

Caro nodded. Of course. How could she have been so thoughtless. 'I'm sorry, Sam.'

He shook his head quickly. 'No, don't say sorry. I had the best day - unexpectedly lovely - *all* of it.'

'Me too,' she said, 'but don't worry, I'll be out of

your hair soon. I'm guessing the roads will have been cleared by now.' She manoeuvred around Sam, picked up the kettle from the Aga and filled the teapot to the brim before replacing the top and popping the cosy on.

'You know, you're welcome to stay a bit longer,' he said quietly. 'I could show you around the village a bit more?'

Caro's heart squeezed and she reached out and took hold of one of Sam's hands, praying he wouldn't pull away.

Sam looked down at their hands then laced his fingers through hers. 'What do you reckon?' he said.

Caro gazed at him. If only she could, but after last night, she knew that it just wouldn't be a good idea. She couldn't risk her heart, could she? She couldn't let anything else happen between them.

'But my parents . . .' she said.

'I could drive you over this evening.'

Caro was so close to giving in, and as he drew her towards him, stroking a loose strand of hair away from her face, she felt her resolve give way.

BEEEEEEEP!

An obnoxiously loud horn out in the yard caused them to jump apart as if a ton of snow had just been dumped on their heads.

'Crap!' squeaked Caro in surprise.

'Who the hell?!' said Sam, half laughing as he darted out of the kitchen to find out was happening.

Caro sighed, and gave herself an impatient shake as

the butterflies in her stomach swooped. Just a moment ago she'd almost managed to convince herself that she didn't want anything more to happen between her and Sam, but now she could quite happily kick whoever was out in the yard for getting in the way of . . . of whatever had just been about to happen.

Heading down the hallway, Caro quickly slipped on her borrowed coat and boots and followed Sam out into the yard to find out what was happening.

'Lyndon, you're a hero!'

Sam's voice drifted back to her as she hurried along the little path. Rounding the corner, she found a huge green tractor sitting in the middle of the yard, and behind it, tethered by a rope, sat Bert. Muddy but looking relatively unscathed.

Caro hurried over. Sam stood chatting with Lyndon, who'd climbed down from his tractor. As she drew nearer a younger guy wearing a blue boilersuit climbed out of Bert's driver's seat.

'Caro, you've met Lyndon,' said Sam as he turned and spotted her.

Caro smiled. 'Of course - thank you so much!'

'No problem - just sorry we couldn't do it for you sooner. This is Jake by the way, my grandson,' he said, gesturing at the youngish looking lad.

'Oh, hi Jake! Thanks for helping!'

'That's okay,' he grinned at her. 'I work over at Bamton motors - I'm going to give the car a quick check-over - just to make sure you're safe.'

'That's so kind!'

Jake shook his head. 'It's no bother,' he grinned, 'I owe Sam a few favours anyway.'

'Hope you've got a decent spare tyre in there, Caro,' said Sam as he moved around the back of Bert. 'You've got a flat - probably a bit of wire or something when you hit the verge.'

Caro pulled a face. 'The spare tyre is brand new - I replaced it during the last MOT - and if that's the only issue you find, I think I got off lightly!'

Jake nodded. 'Sam, mind if I use your barn instead of changing it out here in the snow?'

Sam nodded. The Land Rover was still safely down in the pub car park so Jake unhooked the tow rope and drove Bert straight onto the dry concrete of the barn.

'How about I make us all that cuppa?' Caro asked quietly.

❄

She knew she should be happy that Bert didn't need anything other than a new spare tyre, but as she made the bed in her room for the last time and gathered her things into her pack, Caro felt . . . hollow.

Sam had asked her again if she'd like to spend the rest of the day with him, but now she had Bert back, and the roads were relatively clear, she felt like she had to go.

She hated saying no to him, but she needed to

spend some time with her mum and dad - hell, just a couple of days ago, she couldn't wait to get there. But now, she found she didn't want to leave Little Bamton and her new friends behind. She didn't want to leave Sam. Maybe it was just the last remnants of Christmas spirit making her feel like this - but leaving was inevitable, so there was no point putting it off, was there?

'Want me to take anything down for you?' asked Sam, peering around the door as Caro hefted her pack onto her shoulder.

'My table?' she asked, trailing her fingertips over the glossy surface. 'I still can't believe you gave that to me.'

'I'm just glad you like it,' he said, lifting it easily and following her carefully down the twisting stairs.

They made their way out to the car and Caro indicated for Sam to place her precious table on the back seat as the boot was still packed with the gifts she'd brought along for her family.

Sam secured the table with a seatbelt and was just scrambling out backwards when he paused and bent down.

'What's up?' asked Caro.

'You'll never guess what I've just found,' he said, emerging with a grin and pushing his hair out of his eyes.

'What?' she asked.

Sam held out her errant mobile phone, and she laughed.

'Thanks,' she said quietly, taking it from him. 'Thanks for everything,' she added.

'You too,' he said, catching hold of her hand and pulling her into a hug.

Caro threw her arms around him and held him for a long moment. 'I'll call you?' she said pulling back and patting her pocket that held the scrap of paper with both his and Lucy's phone numbers scrawled on it.

Sam nodded.

'Okay,' she said, opening Bert's door, because she knew that if she didn't leave now, she wouldn't leave at all.

'Drive safe Caro. No more ditches, okay?'

'No more ditches,' she laughed, sliding in behind the wheel and pulling the door closed. She quickly wound down the window. 'Merry Christmas, Sam.'

'Merry Christmas Caro,' he said, patting the top of Bert before stepping back.

The last thing she saw in her rear-view mirror as she pulled out of the yard, was Sam, standing there in the snow, watching her leave.

CHAPTER 17

'Caro love! Merry Christmas,' cried her mum, pulling her into a warm hug that smelled of cinnamon, and that mum-ness that Caro knew so well.

'Merry Christmas mum,' she said. 'I finally made it!'

'Come on in. Your sister's here and I'm sure she could do with a hand wrangling those boys- they're high on sugar and being spoilt rotten.'

'My favourite combination,' laughed Caro as she followed her mum inside.

'Aunty Caro, Aunty Caro! You're late!'

Two small boys pelted down the hallway and wrapped themselves around her legs, making it practically impossible for her to walk. She laughed as she reached down and prized seven-year-old Luke off and hoisted him in the air.

'When did you get so big?!' she laughed, as he squealed in delight.

'Not as big as meeee!' bellowed ten-year-old Tim, refusing point-blank to relinquish her other leg so that she had to hobble towards the sitting room while dragging him along with her.

'Give her a break, boys,' ordered Sandy, Caro's sister as soon as she spotted what was going on. 'Poor old Aunty Caro's had a rubbish Christmas!'

The boys stopped fighting her and instantly hugged her instead like the naughty little angels they were.

Caro sank gratefully into one of the sofas and the boys snuggled into either side of her.

'You know,' she said, 'I actually had a really lovely Christmas.'

'Charming!' huffed her sister.

Caro smirked at her.

'Well,' she continued, 'it was the usual mayhem here. Of course we missed you, though.'

'Thanks sis,' said Caro. She was about to say that she'd missed them too but stopped herself before she opened her mouth. It just wouldn't be honest. Apart from a brief pang of sadness when she'd called her parents from the pub on Christmas day, Caro had been so happy and so wrapped up in everything that was going on around her, she hadn't given a single thought to anything that was going on outside of Little Bamton. She'd felt like she was at home.

She swallowed hard. She was being ridiculous.

'Bet you missed your presents too, didn't you?' she said to the boys, trying to cover up a confusing wave of homesickness for a place she'd only entered for the first time three days ago.

The boys instantly started clamouring for their gifts and wouldn't let up until she went back to the car to fetch them.

'Where's mum and dad?' she asked Sandy, after handing over a parcel to each of the boys and watching while they tore into them like miniature whirlwinds.

'Getting ready for their guests, I guess,' said Sandy with a shrug.

'Guests?' For one brilliant, completely insane moment, Caro imagined everyone from Little Bamton descending on the house. Alf, Lucy, Sue, Lyndon, the vicar . . . Sam. It was official, she was losing the plot!

'Yeah - you know, the usuals. Uncle Derek, the guys from down the road who always bring turkey curry that stinks the place out for a week, dad's friends from the metal detecting club, mum's bridge partners . . . and any other randoms she's bumped into and taken pity on.' Her sister chuckled and rolled her eyes.

Caro's heart sank. How could she had been so wrapped up in herself that she'd forgotten her parents' Boxing Day Open House. Today was Boxing Day, so of course it was happening!

She'd been so focused on getting back here to spend time with her family today, she'd managed to forget that - in just an hour or so - the place would fill up with dozens of people, and she'd be stuck handing around plates filled with cheese and pineapple chunks on sticks.

'Now boys, say thanks to Aunty Caro!' Sandy ordered, and Caro's attention landed firmly back in the room as the two lads began an epic dino-fight on the carpet with the massive plastic dinosaurs she'd given them.

'Thank you Aunty Caro!' they both yelled and, jumping to their feet, they began to pummel her with the toys.

Great. *Great.* She was already secretly regretting giving up a cosy day exploring Little Bamton with Sam - for *this*.

She wondered if he'd sent her a text yet, and then promptly loathed herself for even thinking about it. She'd only left an hour ago! Maybe she'd just quickly pop her phone on to charge though - the battery was flatter than flat after three nights playing Christmas songs in a ditch.

❉

An hour later, the Open House was in full swing and there were people everywhere. Caro didn't know many of them, and the few she did, she was doing her best to avoid because all they wanted to do was ask her about her love life, and whether her "lovely boyfriend" was there with her. Clearly they hadn't got the memo about Gareth being the world's biggest prat.

She'd just managed to escape a nice but intensely boring friend of her dad's who was intent on giving her advice on choosing the best metal detector for a beginner, when her mum beckoned her into the kitchen.

'Caro love, would you mind taking the turkey curry and dips through to the dining room for me?' she said, taking a sneaky peek around her before leaning in and whispering, 'the smell's burning my nose!'

Caro laughed and took the dish of what looked like toxic waste out of her mum's hands. Holding it at arm's length, she marched it through to the sitting room and deposited it safely on the table.

She was just about to retreat back towards the kitchen, hoping for a few minutes with her parents, when Uncle Derek accosted her by the door.

'How's your lovely man, Caro?' he asked, chomping on a handful of Twiglets.

'Oh, uh . . . I . . .' Not this again! Her eyes darted around until she spotted her phone sitting on the sideboard, still attached its charger. 'Sorry Uncle Derek,' she said making a dive for it, 'I've got an urgent call to make. Be right back!'

She slid open the glass patio doors, squeezed out into the garden and pulled them shut again behind her.

Gah! It was freezing out here. Never mind, better a little bit of frostbite than the love-life third degree for what felt like the thousandth time today.

Caro marched off across the snowy lawn and rounded the corner into her dad's tiny but perfectly formed veg patch. She couldn't help but smile as the sight of the little greenhouse and raised beds, complete with the occasional unidentified dead stalk, reminded her of the allotments back in Little Bamton.

She sighed. She really wished she'd stayed there now. Looking down, Caro quickly hit the power button on her phone and held her breath. Would there be a message?

She stamped her feet and hugged herself while she waited for it to find a signal. Goodness it was cold. She wasn't going to be able to stay out here for long.

The phone vibrated several times in her hand as a flurry of notifications popped up. She quickly opened up her texts, only to find that most of them were round-robin messages from various uni friends and old work colleagues wishing everyone in their phone books a Merry Christmas.

As she clicked through them, one by one, her heart sank with disappointment. Of course there wasn't one from Sam. Not yet. A small voice in the back of her mind whispered *maybe never*, and she felt a lump form in her throat.

'Pull it together!' she muttered to herself out loud, her breath pluming in the cold air. She really should go back in. Maybe she'd just check her emails while she was out here too - anything to avoid having to go back to Uncle Derek already.

It was just the usual rubbish, a mixture of offers for

penile enlargements, and various newsletters - most of which she had no memory of signing up for.

Caro flipped the cover closed and slid her phone into her back pocket. It was time for round two of *Where's Your Perfect Boyfriend*.

❄

Half an hour later, Caro found herself standing sandwiched between the two turkey curry guys, holding a half-full plate of cheese and pineapple chunks on sticks while pretending to listen to their discussion on how to make the perfect turkey curry. She was just wondering how best to escape when she felt her phone buzz in her back pocket and nearly managed to impale one of them with her collection of cocktail sticks.

'Erm, would you excuse for me a moment?' she asked, cutting one of them off mid-sentence as he was extolling the virtues of adding left-over raspberry jam to the recipe. She handed him the plate and scooted off up the stairs as fast as she could.

Mercifully the bathroom was empty, so she locked herself in and perched on the edge of the bath.

Damn, it was just an email. She'd been certain for some reason that it would be Sam. She quickly opened it up - and a huge grin spread across her face.

It was from the Mark, Little Bamton's vicar. True to his word, he'd sent her the details of the empty unit at the craft centre. A swoop of excitement went through her as she glanced through the details.

Did she dare? If this Christmas had taught her anything, it was that wonderful things could happen when you least expected them to - and that change could be a blessing.

She hit "reply", typed out a quick response and sent it before she could chicken out.

Caro stood up as if to head back down to the party, but promptly sat back down again. If she was going to do this properly, there was a call she needed to make. She felt around in her jeans pockets and then pulled out the scrap of paper with the two phone numbers on it. She stared at the top one for a long moment before dialling.

'Lucy? Hi, it's Caro. I've had an idea . . .'

❄

Caro couldn't stop grinning as she watched the snow-capped hedges whizz by. Every time she pictured the surprise on her mum's face when she'd announced that she was *"sorry but, she had somewhere important to be"*, she let out a giggle.

She loved her parents very much, but she wasn't quite so keen on their Boxing Day Open House and their ability to gather quite so many truly boring people into one space. Never mind - Caro had plans to make some big changes in her life, and avoiding

Boxing Day Open House next year was high on her list.

She indicated and turned Bert carefully onto a narrow country lane, forcing herself not to bounce in her seat with excitement. She couldn't believe she was doing this - but here she was.

She navigated her way down to the two hump-back bridges and turned right, grinning as she spotted the white lights of Little Bamton at Christmas laid out in front of her.

'I'm home,' she said aloud, then let out a little squeal of excitement when she spotted Sue walking along the pavement with a group of kids. She waved at them, and Sue waved back, a look of surprise on her smiling face.

Flump!

Caro jumped and laughed as one of the lads lobbed a snowball at Bert as she drove past.

Just up ahead was the little square, with the church, the pub, the craft centre and the allotments, but that wasn't where she was headed. At least, not yet.

Later on tonight, she had her official trial shift at the pub to look forward to, and Lucy had promised to show her around the flat upstairs. Tomorrow, she was meeting the Vicar for a proper look around her new unit at the craft centre. But right now, she had somewhere even more important to be.

She indicated again and turned Bert onto the same steep hill she'd taken a gamble on the night of her birthday. Mercifully, the roads had been cleared and gritted, but she still kept it slow. No matter how much she wanted to push her foot to the floor - there was no way she wanted to end up in the ditch again.

The lights of Sam's cabin shone like a welcoming beacon as she turned back into the yard she'd only left that morning. As she parked up and killed the engine, Caro couldn't help the ball of nerves that suddenly filled her stomach. Was this okay? Well, there was only one way to find out!

Climbing out of the car, Caro drew Lucy's red coat tightly around her, took a deep breath and made her way to the back door of the cabin.

She paused, and then rang the bell.

Nothing.

Complete silence.

Crap.

Disappointment filled the space where her nerves had been just moments before. No, this wasn't right. She had to see Sam. She gently tried the door handle and, to her surprise, it opened.

'Sam?' she called, sticking her head around the door.

Nothing.

She tried again, this time a little louder, but there was still no answer.

Caro turned and closed the door behind her. Surely he must be around here somewhere if he'd left the cabin unlocked?

She followed the path around to where his workshop stood, still covered in its blanket of snow. The door was open.

There were those nerves again!

Caro made her way over and peered in quietly.

Sam was working at the bench, a fine piece of sandpaper in his hand. She watched his face. He was so intent on his work that he hadn't spotted her yet.

Caro glanced down at the bench and gasped as he drew his hand away and blew the fine dust off the carving of a beautiful angel. Amy's angel. He'd finished it.

'What are you doing back here?' he asked, making her jump. Her eyes flew back to his face, which was now turned towards her. She was dreading to find anger there, but instead there was just complete surprise.

Caro paused, her excitement taking a moment to battle with the pure fear that maybe she shouldn't be here after all.

'Bert's not back in the ditch is he?' he demanded, the corner of his mouth lifting in the start of a smile.

Caro shook her head, allowing a small smile to creep onto her own face.

'I forgot something,' she said.

'Oh.' Sam looked a little taken aback and got to his feet. 'What is it? Do you want to go into the cabin to look for it? It's open . . .'

'I know. I already looked. It wasn't in there.'

'Well I . . .'

'It's here,' she said, coming to stand right in front of him.

'Here?' he said, looking confused.

'I think so . . . isn't it?' she asked, raising her eyebrows and holding his gaze. 'Aren't you?' she added quietly.

Sam stared at her for a long, breathless moment. Then he looked back down at the angel on the bench. He ran a gentle finger over the soft curves of its beautiful face before turning back to her.

'I am,' he replied, his voice low. Reaching out, he brushed a loose strand of hair away from her face.

Caro slowly wrapped her arms around him, her heart starting to hammer as his warmth and the scent of wood shavings and beeswax washed over her.

Sam wrapped one arm around her waist and twined his other hand gently into her hair before slowly bringing his face down to hers.

Caro closed her eyes as his lips kissed her gently on the forehead before finally meeting hers in the softest of Christmas kisses.

THE END

ALSO BY BETH RAIN

Little Bamton Series:

Little Bamton: The Complete Series Collection: Books 1 - 5

Individual titles:

Christmas Lights and Snowball Fights (Little Bamton Book 1)

Spring Flowers and April Showers (Little Bamton Book 2)

Summer Nights and Pillow Fights (Little Bamton Book 3)

Autumn Cuddles and Muddy Puddles (Little Bamton Book 4)

Christmas Flings and Wedding Rings (Little Bamton Book 5)

Upper Bamton Series:

A New Arrival in Upper Bamton (Upper Bamton Book 1)

Rainy Days in Upper Bamton (Upper Bamton Book 2)

Hidden Treasures in Upper Bamton (Upper Bamton Book 3)

Time Flies By in Upper Bamton (Upper Bamton Book 4)

Seabury Series:

Welcome to Seabury (Seabury Book 1)

Trouble in Seabury (Seabury Book 2)

Christmas in Seabury (Seabury Book 3)

Sandwiches in Seabury (Seabury Book 4)

Secrets in Seabury (Seabury Book 5)

Surprises in Seabury (Seabury Book 6)

Dreams and Ice Creams in Seabury (Seabury Book 7)

Mistakes and Heartbreaks in Seabury (Seabury Book 8)

Laughter and Happy Ever After in Seabury (Seabury Book 9)

Seabury Series Collections:

Kate's Story: Books 1 - 3

Hattie's Story: Books 4 - 6

Writing as Bea Fox:

What's a Girl To Do? The Complete Series

Individual titles:

The Holiday: What's a Girl To Do? (Book 1)

The Wedding: What's a Girl To Do? (Book 2)

The Lookalike: What's a Girl To Do? (Book 3)

The Reunion: What's a Girl To Do? (Book 4)

At Christmas: What's a Girl To Do? (Book 5)

ABOUT THE AUTHOR

Beth Rain has always wanted to be a writer and has been penning adventures for characters ever since she learned to stare into the middle-distance and daydream.

She currently lives in the (sometimes) sunny South West, and it is a dream come true to spend her days hanging out with Bob – her trusty laptop – scoffing crisps and chocolate while dreaming up swoony love stories for all her imaginary friends.

Beth's writing will always deliver on the happy-ever-afters, so if you need cosy… you're in safe hands!

Visit www.bethrain.com for all the bookish goodness and keep up with all Beth's news by joining her monthly newsletter!

- facebook.com/BethRainBooks
- twitter.com/bethrainauthor
- instagram.com/bethrainauthor

Printed in Great Britain
by Amazon